GO HOME BLACKIE

GROWING UP BLACK IN BRITAIN IN THE FIFTIES AND SIXTIES

M P APPLETON

CONTENTS

PROLOGUE

My mother and I were on a bus going to Kentish Town. We were going to Mass. My mother was a devout strict Catholic and we never missed Mass on Sunday because it would be a mortal sin and our entry into Heaven would be denied.

As we prepared to step off the bus a loud strident angry voice rang out behind us.

"GO HOME BLACKIE."

I turned and saw a woman staring malevolently at us as we made our way to the platform. She looked crazed, her eyes flashing wildly, her lips a snarl. I was scared and reached for my mother's hand. There was no doubt her words were aimed at us. We were the only *coloured* people on the bus (*coloured* was how we were politely referred to in those days).

My mother held my hand tightly and as the bus slowed we jumped down before it came to a complete stop. It was as though she was trying to get away, as quickly as possible, from the angry woman. I looked back and met the mad eyes of the woman now standing on the platform of the bus as she continued to shout about, *our country,* followed by words sounding very much like, *swinging from trees.*

As the bus pulled away from the bus stop, the woman standing on the platform was waving a fist and shouting something I could no longer hear. Everyone on the bus stared at us, their blank indifferent faces frightened me. Had we done something wrong?

I clung to my mother's hand terrified something was going to happen to us. The woman on the bus looked as though she was preparing to jump down and come after us.

My mother looked straight ahead her teeth chewing anxiously on her lower lip. I was puzzled at her lack of reaction. Why didn't she say something?

"Mama, what did we do?" I asked as my mother determinedly pulled me along in her wake towards Our Lady Help of Christians.

"Hurry," she gasped ignoring my question and breaking into a run. "If we don't get there before the gospel finishes we will have missed Mass."

All thoughts of the angry woman quickly evaporated as the fear of missing Mass transcended all else.

Missing Mass on a Sunday was unthinkable. What would we do? I picked up my pace and ran beside her, my legs straining to keep up.

The twelve Mass on Sunday was the last mass of the day. I trembled with trepidation, not only from the fear of committing a mortal sin but from the genuine and present dread that Sister Agatha might find out during assembly the next day. The cane would be Sister Agatha's inevitably punishment.

"Quick." My mother urged me on. I looked up and saw anxiety on her face and lengthened my stride.

At the church door, she pushed through the crowd of parishioners spilling out onto the pavement. As we stepped over the threshold she gave a sigh of relief.

"We've made it," she whispered.

It was hot and airless standing at the back of the church jammed together with the other latecomers. Being small, I couldn't see a thing. The stale smell of cigarette smoke and body sweat wafted around me and I felt sick. I rose on tiptoe and peered between bodies to see Father Fitzgerald close the large ornate bible, make the sign of the cross in preparation to start his sermon and then pause. He stood tall in the pulpit and looked around.

"Come up to the front," he shouted waving his hands at those of us standing at the back. "There are plenty of seats down here in the front rows."

I cringed as my mother pulled me down the aisle to the front. We clambered over legs as people shifted to make space for us.

Father Fitzgerald looked satisfied as other sheepish looking parishioners filled the last few remaining places in the front pews. His eyes returned to the back of the church still crowded and people hung their heads as they shuffled their feet.

"Back home." His voice rang out. "We would get to Mass on time and not insult the Lord by being late. You wouldn't be late to a friend's party now would you?"

I gasped. *Home*, he'd said. If we weren't home, where were we? I looked up at my mother, longing to ask her.

Go home. I thought of the woman on the bus. I fidgeted, squirming in my seat, where was our home? How would we go back home if we didn't know where home was?

As the last prayers were said, my mother grabbed my hand and we rushed out of the church before the priest left the altar.

"I think we will walk home today." She looked nervous. I suspected getting on a bus again frightened her and so had decided to walk home, despite it being a long way.

"Why did the woman on the bus tell us to go home?"

I slipped my hand into hers and we walked in silence for sometime before she answered. "You mustn't worry. There are people who don't like *coloured* people."

"But where is our home?" I persisted.

"We are home. Don't worry about what the woman on the bus said. This is our home Harmony."

Being called *Blackie*, wasn't unusual. I got called *Blackie* often, at school, walking home from school or wherever I happen to be. I never got used to it, but it happened regularly, so I accepted it was part of being *coloured*.

3

It made me sad when people called me names like *Blackie, monkey face* or *nigger*. I couldn't understand what difference our colour made, but it seemed to matter a lot to some people.

The angry woman's words, *Go home blackie,* stayed with me for years. I often wondered where we would go if we had to go home? Where would my home be?

CHAPTER 1

I was born three weeks earlier than expected, on the twenty-ninth of January at twelve-thirty, on one of the coldest winter nights my parents could remember.

My birth took place in war-torn Coventry, whilst my father stood outside the door of our rented one-roomed home, on the top floor of a tall lodging house filled with sleeping tenants.

My mother was eternally proud of the way she pushed me into the world and frequently boasted she had made no sound, barely a grunt, though she has since admitted she suffered the worst pain she'd ever experienced.

Her stoicism was not for any altruistic reason, but out of fear. She was afraid of disturbing the other occupants of the house...worried should there be any complaint about noise, the landlord would take the opportunity to evict them, since he hadn't wanted *coloured* tenants in the first place.

My mother had searched the streets of Coventry looking for somewhere to live and had seen a notice in the window advertising a room for rent. She and my father needed somewhere to live desperately. She was tenacious and never gave up when she wanted something badly enough, and finding somewhere to live was one of those occasions.

"We have to try," she said when my father had pointed out the small poster and its conditions to her. Ignoring the conditions of renting she climbed the steps to the front door and raised the heavy knocker.

Surprise had shown on the landlord's face as on opening the door he found himself facing a woman, a *coloured* woman. She asked if she could rent the room he was advertising in his window. Silently he pointed to the small handwritten poster, ROOM FOR RENT NO COLOUREDS NO IRISH.

She looked at him and asked him why? He didn't know why at least he couldn't articulate why except he'd heard bad things about *coloured* people.

He had been curious about her. "Where do you come from?"

"My father was English," she told him and saw surprise followed swiftly by pity swim into his eyes. She knew being *half-caste* was seen as warranting pity, something she never understood, but if it got her a home she didn't care. She'd always been proud of her parentage, loved being both African and English, and could never understand why others pitied her.

The landlord looked as though he was about to close the door but had hesitated and she had taken advantage of his hesitation and begged him to reconsider.

" I wouldn't mind renting to you," he said finally. "But my other tenants wouldn't like *coloured* people in the house and I don't want trouble."

She pleaded with him, and he eventually agreed to rent them the room as long as they didn't disturb the other tenants. There was a recently vacated room at the top of the house, he told them as he stepped back to allow them to enter.

Why he changed his mind was debatable. Maybe her unusual beauty had intrigued him, her large dark brown eyes or her skin as smooth and the colour of pale honey may have fascinated him. She was, after all, almost one of them...well, half one of them.

Maybe seeing the advanced state of her pregnancy and that it was just before Christmas, had reminded him of another family, Joseph and Mary. They too had trouble finding a room. Maybe he thought my mother and father looked as though they'd fallen on hard times, and he'd felt sorry for them. Then again, maybe, under the hard exterior of his prejudice, he was, after all, a compassionate man. Whatever the reason, he relented.

Though small, the room was gratefully accepted and my mother immediately set about turning it into a home for her, soon to be, little family.

They were lucky, the landlord told them, the toilet was only two flights down and the shared kitchen was only one flight down. He told them cooking was not allowed, after nine at night.

He mentioned her pregnancy and said if he let them have the room, her baby mustn't disturb the other tenants. My mother put her hand protectively on her stomach and assured him her baby would be very quiet. As you can imagine, from then on, she lived in constant fear of being made homeless.

CHAPTER 2

My father was home at the time of my birth. He was a dance-band singer and was resting. In showbiz speak, he was out of work and was looking to join another dance-band. Not having been able to afford an overcoat, he'd padded himself with old newspapers under his shirt and jacket to keep warm when dispatched into the night to fetch the midwife.

It was snowing heavily. Snowflakes large and thick floated down relentlessly, turning the dark streets of Coventry into a white fairy-land where the dingy world of bombed out houses glistened magi-cally. Through the darkness of the snowy winter's night, my father trudged across town leaving footsteps in the crisp glistening snow. The falling snow covered his shoes and settled on his jacket soaking through to the newspapers surrounding his torso.

There were no streetlights. Blackouts were mandatory in Great Britain in the last months of the war with Germany, and in order to disorientate the German bombers, the city was thrown into total blackness. Not even a chink of light escaped from the darkened windows to offer him a clue he was heading in the right direction.

Shadowy edifices of tall blacked-out houses and snow-covered rubble, the remnants of homes destroyed in bombing raids, lined the streets. He made his way towards the midwife's lodgings frequently disorientated, as every street looked the same. In his panic he found himself retracing his steps again and again in his search. The relief he felt when at last he arrived quickly evaporated when he discovered the midwife was out attending to another birth.

Worried, he left a quickly scribbled note and ran back to find my mother in excruciating pain gripping the side of the bed and panting rapidly. Her waters had broken, and she feared my birth was imminent.

"We're going to need hot water," she gasped as my father rushed into the room. Between gasps, she instructed him to scrub up, boil the kettle, fill what saucepans he could find with water and boil those too. She had been a midwife before they'd met, so knew what to do. He grabbed what receptacles he could find, a halfpenny for the gas meter and rushed down to the kitchen.

My father anxiously flittered around as the kettle whistled and the saucepans of water bubbled away on top of the stove. He kept rushing up and down the stairs returning with pans of boiling water, which he placed on the hearth.

With sleeves rolled up he looked on in awe as my mother raised her legs and said, "I have to push."

It was then the midwife arrived. She bustled in, removed her coat and hat, stood at the end of the bed and spoke sternly to my mother. "Don't push yet, I need to examine you."

She turned to look at my father, took in his rolled-up sleeves and raised an eyebrow. "Out, out," she enunciated bossily. "We won't be needing you. You can wait out there." She pointed to the door and turned to my mother. "Don't push yet. Wait."

My father stepped onto the landing and the door was shut firmly behind him. And so the stage was set for my birth.

As I slid into the world my legs were grasped tightly, I was swung upside down and given a resounding slap on my bottom before being swaddled tightly in a knitted blanket and placed in a drawer prepared for me. My parents hadn't been able to afford a cot and so, I was placed in a drawer next to the coal fire.

"A bonny baby girl," the midwife said smiling. "What are you going to call her?"

I was given the name of Harmony. Yes, Harmony, a misnomer if ever there was one, as I was frequently told I would try the patience of a Saint.

CHAPTER 3

Apart from an early memory of my mother getting angry with me, and swooning to the floor in a faint and not gaining consciousness until I'd apologised, my childhood, at home was fairly unremarkable. But outside of home, things were very different.

There was the time when I was eight years old and Sister Agatha caned me for making my sampler dirty because she said I had omitted to wash my dirty hands after coming in from play. It was then I realized for the first time, I was different, really different, different in a way I could do nothing about. And being different was a major disability in the eyes of those around me, particularly Sister Agatha.

It all happened on a bitterly cold winter's day after we had been shepherded out to the playground for fifteen minutes of unadulterated torture, called Playtime. It was agony trying to keep warm as we shivered in the damp, cramped play area until the end of playtime. We ran to line up in our class groups to wait until our teacher fresh from the warm staffroom, marched us back to class in an angry silence. Our teachers always appeared angry, and this had the effect of making me feel perpetually anxious.

"Make sure you've washed your hands," Sister Martha Mary, our teacher said as we were marched inside to hang our coats on our assigned pegs.

I took off my gloves and looked at my hands. They were clean and anyway it was too late now. The toilet block was out back, removed from the main classroom building and we got into trouble if we asked to go to the toilet during lessons. Then again, I knew the icy water would cause more pain to my swollen chilblained fingers, something I preferred to avoid.

I dared not think of what would happen if I asked to wash my hands after playtime, so I gave it a miss and stood in line behind Kathleen Maloney of the long dark hair and squeaky voice.

Once inside, I took off my coat and slipped quickly into the classroom making sure to pass the large coal-fired stove on my way to my desk. As I passed, I briefly held out my hands to soak in some warmth.

This was our weekly sewing lesson and I looked forward to it. We weren't allowed to talk during our sewing lesson but I didn't mind because this lesson didn't involve getting the cane for not being able to answer questions. I wasn't required to know my tables, nor recite the Catechism, it was bliss. I sat focused on my little sampler, needle and thread in hand. All I had to do was guide a short stubby needle threaded with red embroidery cotton in and out of a piece of material. It was a period in my school life when I felt safe. I loved those lessons and thought my sampler looked wonderful.

On this occasion, a tall shadow fell across the threshold as Sister Agatha pushed open the door and came to stand alongside our teacher, Sister Martha Mary. We all rose from our seats as expected and chanted as was mandatory, "Good Morning Sister Agatha."

Tension filled the air as it always did when Sister Agatha appeared. Sister Martha Mary, her short round stubby figure shrouded in black, her round pink face encased tightly in a wimple accentuating watery blue eyes and spiky grey chin hairs, quivered at the mere appearance of Sister Agatha.

Although Sister Martha Mary wasn't particularly nice to me and though she only seemed to smile at Mary Murphy, her favourite, I felt sorry for her. I suppose the compassion I felt for her was due to our shared nemesis...Sister Agatha.

"Is everything all right Sister Martha Mary?" Sister Agatha asked loudly her brow furrowed as her hawk-like eyes whirled around the classroom.

Sister Martha Mary gave a nervous smile, looked anxiously at us, nodded and murmured, "Yes Sister." She sounded more hopeful than convinced.

Sister Agatha looked none too pleased with the lack of problems. She turned towards us and started to walk up and down between the rows of desks, stopping every few steps to peer closely at someone's embroidery.

"Very good Eileen," she said to Eileen Clark and moved on.

The air was filled with the scent of unbridled fear, we all knew her appearance heralded castigation and physical pain for someone. But who was it to be this time?

We were in the process of learning to cross-stitch and the red embroidery thread looked wonderful crisscrossing around the edge of the sampler...in and out...in and out.

I'd worked really hard, diligently counting the holes before I stuck the needle into the thick weave of the sampler and then counted carefully before I pushed the needle back up, crossing it over and poking it back down again.

The lesson was made even more enjoyable because the boys weren't there. They had already gone to the class next door for something called woodwork and in exchange, we had the girls from the next class to join us for needlework.

"I hope we are all doing some good work and not chatting," Sister Agatha said to us as she reached the front of the class.

Her eyes darted quickly around the room once more, then fell on me. A sliver of fear slid ominously down my spine and I shivered and quickly lowered my eyes returning my attention to my sampler. I was cold, so very cold, and I was filled with dread as I felt something menacing hover over me. Yet I was unprepared for what was to follow.

"You," Sister Agatha's voice boomed out and I looked up to see who the unfortunate girl she had picked out was to be, only to find she was pointing a long finger directly at me.

"Jesus, Mary and Joseph. Were you not told to wash your hands before you came to class?" She took a step towards me.

"Sister, did you not tell them?" She demanded turning towards our teacher. Sister Martha Mary nodded vigorously, her wimple quivering, her lips barely moving in the whispered, "Yes, Sister."

Obviously, Sister Agatha didn't believe Sister Martha Mary because she turned to the class.

"Did Sister Martha Mary not remind you to wash your hands before class?"

Everyone nodded as they replied in unison, "Yes, Sister Agatha."

Sister Martha Mary looked visibly relieved because, in all honesty, she and I and the rest of the girls knew she had not reminded us before play, although it was an understood rule dished out at the very beginning of the school year. She had mentioned washing our hands only as we were returning to class and then, we all knew it was too late.

I didn't answer. Sister Agatha turned to me once more and my eyes met pale blue pinpricks of anger. I held my breath and my grip tightened on my needle. She stepped forward.

"Come up here at once and bring your filthy rag with you."

From somewhere out of the folds of her long black skirt, a cane appeared like magic. Who would have thought a cane could have been concealed so effectively in a nun's habit? How could a person whose clothing, meant to represent a life of compassion and love, in the name of Jesus Christ, secrete such an instrument of torture?

"Hold out your hand." Her lips thinned as her face took on a look akin to satisfaction. Sister Agatha gave me six of the best with the cane, all the while telling me my sampler was so dirty it looked as though it belonged in the coalhouse.

She bared her teeth. "And you with it." She snatched the sampler out of my hand and held it high for all to see.

"It doesn't take an idiot..." she barked (when she said idiot, it sounded like, idjut), "...to work out you, Harmony Brown did not wash your hands before the lesson."

Bending over me like a large crow intending to peck my eyes out, the sleeves of her habit seemingly winged, flapped as she slapped the cane on the nearest desk and glared at me. "Did you not understand what Sister Martha Mary said?"

"Yes...No," I stuttered. Did she want an answer? I trembled, nodded and then shook my head in confusion.

Sister Agatha went on to say something about my black hands needing extra washing as she poked me in the chest with the tip of the cane. "Go back to your desk and take this filthy rag with you."

I stretched my hand out to receive the sampler I had been enjoying so much but now had lost its enchantment. I didn't care if I never saw it again.

"You and your piece of rag are certainly not white." She held my sampler between her thumb and index finger and dropped it onto my palm as though she could scarcely stand to touch it.

"I'll be watching you next time Harmony Brown," She hissed, turned and walked towards the door where she stood looking briefly over her shoulder to throw me a look dripping with hate. I cowered back in my desk.

How? You may ask, at the tender age of eight, did I know what hate looked like?

Easy, you only had to be black in England in the nineteen fifties where it wasn't unusual for people to shout abuse at you. Oh yes, it was easy to recognise hate.

As Sister Agatha left and shut the classroom door with a decisive click, I sighed with relief. We all sat silent. I watched as Maureen O' Sullivan, the needle monitor, collected the needles and samplers and threw them carelessly into a box, to be brought out at the next sewing lesson when I knew, if Sister Agatha had anything to do with it, I would be punished again, for making my already dirty sampler, dirty.

CHAPTER 4

After the incident of the sampler, Sister Agatha was particularly vigilant where I was concerned. Her eyes constantly sort me out in order to hold me up as a bad example and to punish me for being such.

And I was right. When it happened again, I couldn't hold my tongue. I had a strong sense of fairness and couldn't tolerate what I considered as an injustice. Being only eight years old and impulsive, I sought retaliation. Sniffing defiantly I held my head high when she told me to hold my hand out. The words slipped out as she readied the cane to strike me for some imagined transgression.

"When I grow up, I'm not going to be a Catholic."

There was a heartbeat of silence as the words left my lips. The cane hovered in the air and a deep hush settled on the class as though the world had, rather unexpectedly, come to an end.

My dark brown eyes defiantly held blue watery eyes, and I saw a momentary flash of disbelief quickly followed by unmitigated rage.

A split second of reprieve before the cane came whooshing down with such force, it split my already chilblain swollen fingers and caused blood to seep onto my palm. I winced biting back a cry as it rose to my lips. Though I was suffering excruciating pain and felt dizzy, a mixture of fear and at the same time exhilaration at my daring, flooded through me.

I didn't care what happened to me. I was angry and incensed, even the pain of my fingers, cut and bleeding receded as I felt a power I had never felt before. I had made this woman angry, so angry she'd been struck dumb for a moment. I felt powerful. I knew I had won, and knowing was satisfaction indeed.

Had Sister Agatha put me to death there and then I wouldn't have cared an iota. I knew instinctively what martyrs must have felt like at the point of death...powerful.

"You bold, wicked girl," Sister Agatha shrieked pulling herself together and finding her voice. Her face reddened alarmingly, her wimple quivered, and she demanded I hold out my hand again for six more of her punishment best.

I hesitated confused. Sister Agatha had called me bold. Wasn't *bold* a good thing to be? I'd always thought we were meant to be bold as opposed to cowardly, but the way the cane was raised above me indicated, I'd somehow got it wrong. Being bold was something bad and as the cane fell once more across my fingers, I began to understand, I *had* got it wrong, badly wrong.

Sister Agatha struggled for breath between the exertions of her canning and shrieking I was a very wicked girl. Moreover, she said she was forced to punish me, in order to ensure I remained forever faithful to the Church.

She took in a deep breath and added for good measure, "I will not have a heathen in my school. So now you can collect your coat and go home. Tell your mother you want to be a heathen."

Fear engulfed me. I stood my ground and fought to hold back the tears threatening to spill down my face. I couldn't imagine telling my mother any such thing in case she collapsed in a faint and failed to recover. Being Catholic was very important to her. Being a Catholic was her identity, the only identity she had after being abandoned in a Catholic convent, by her Colonial Officer father, at the age of seven. He had died suddenly and no one had come for her.

I forced air into my lungs now tight with terror. Yet I was determined Sister Agatha wouldn't see how frightened I was at the prospect of returning home in the middle of the day. Besides, there would be no one at home and I would have to sit on the doorstep until my mother returned from work. My father was away in Margate, performing at the Winter Gardens and wouldn't be home for a few weeks.

Bravado spurred me on. What did I have to lose? I felt a sense of power. As my hand reached for the door handle, I turned and glanced quickly over my shoulder and met laser-sharp eyes as they contracted into slits behind her thick lenses warning me there was more to come. I threw my head back defiantly, flicked my plaits off my shoulders and jutted my chin out, determined to show Sister Agatha I didn't care about her threats. I wasn't afraid. Not true, I did care and I was afraid, I was terrified. I held my head high, and I marched bravely to the cloakroom to collect my coat, a navy blue woollen coat. It was warm, and I needed the comforting warmth it offered.

My heart was nearly bursting out of my chest in terror as I made my way back into the classroom. I was conscious of Sister Agatha tightly gripping the cane and I shook with dread. Would she cane me again? My chilblains felt as though they were on fire and I squeezed my hand into an even tighter fist.

My classmates were silent as they waited with drawn breath for what would happen next. Like me, they too were afraid. The sound of the cane slapping against the material of her heavy woollen skirt, reminded us all it was itching, just itching, to come into contact with skin, and no doubt, by the look in Sister Agatha's eyes, my *coloured* skin.

The relentless whooshing of the cane glancing off the heavy black material of her long skirt, coupled with the clicking of the large wooden rosary beads as they glided through the fingers of her other hand, rendered me almost paralyzed. I had to force my limbs to move.

It was strange she held onto the rosary in her moment of impenetrable cruelty and to my eight-year-old understanding of life and justice, it was incomprehensible. Was this what nuns did? Did God send them to punish us for our sins? Was this their job on earth? If so, did God hate me too? And if he did, why did he hate me so much? Was it because I wasn't white?

Sister Agatha watched my every move with the silent poise of a cobra stilling before a strike. Her lips shaped into a thin unforgiving line terrified me. For the first time in my few short years on this earth, I felt as though my life was in danger.

The patent strength of her hate hovering like a ball of fire radiating from her, threatening to engulf me, frightened me... truly terrified me.

"Go." She pointed the cane at the door.

My coat tightly buttoned, I turned and looked back as I made my way to the door. Startled, I saw an expression of something new on her face, a look I recognized as, expectation. And I understood instinctively, she wanted me to cry and beg for her forgiveness... I knew I could never give her that satisfaction.

She wanted my capitulation in front of the forty pairs of eyes trained on me in horror, all expecting to witness my immediate demise.

I bit down hard on the inside of my lip until I tasted blood. Never, never, I vowed, as I clenched my fists to my side, would I ever give her the satisfaction of showing my fear. I would rather die. Sister Agatha had no idea who she was dealing with. On this occasion, I preferred to be a martyr. After all martyrs, we'd been taught, preferred to die for what they knew was right. Martyrs never gave in. I wasn't good enough to be a saint, but I could be a martyr.

"Come here you bold girl," she hissed as my hand reached out for the door handle. She leaned towards me as I turned. Her eyes had shrunk into two little orbs and two round red patches appeared on her cheeks.

"God has decided to give you another chance. He doesn't want you to die a heathen like the other black children in Africa."

Those were the days when black was a nasty word...like being called *nigger*...yet she was referring to me as black...it was meant to be an insult. We black people were always politely referred to as *coloured*... a word used as a sort of apology for our unfortunate condition.

CHAPTER 5

I was surprised God had decided to forgive me. I hadn't been out of the classroom for more than a couple of minutes collecting my coat, yet in such a short time, Sister Agatha had been in communication with God.

It seemed whilst I'd been slipping into my coat forcing buttons into buttonholes, God had decided to forgive me without my asking. I didn't want pity, and neither did I want forgiveness. God, as far as I was concerned, was unfair. He only liked white people. It was clear he liked people like Sister Agatha. She was his emissary.

I decided if Sister Agatha wanted me to look sad, I could try. But I wasn't going to cry, never, never would she see me cry. I didn't want to go home alone, as I didn't want my mother to feel I had let her down. It was important to her we fitted in, not draw attention to being *coloured*. I lowered my eyes and stared at her shoes, large shiny black lace-ups with thick heels. Really ugly shoes... her shoes squeaked as she walked.

My father had once told me when shoes squeaked it meant their owner had not paid for them. Clearly, Sister Agatha hadn't paid for her shoes, and they were protesting.

Such were my thoughts as her tirade, detailing my wickedness

21

flowed towards and over me. She was at great pains to impress upon me how, despite my being a bold evil girl, God was a good and merciful father. And even though I had angered him by my wicked ways, I was lucky not to have to die a heathen.

Sister Agatha went on to explain it was fortunate I was already a Catholic because unlike all those ignorant black babies in Africa with no choice, they would have to go to Limbo. "You, on the other hand, won't even have the option of Limbo. Purgatory or Hell will be your only choice if you don't repent. Do you understand?"

We'd been told Limbo was a place without pain or joy and as such, could be considered better than Hell, but was in no way as good as Heaven. I was being told I wouldn't even get into Limbo. I shuddered. Purgatory was a bit like prison, where souls were sent after death to suffer punishing flames to cleanse their souls before being allowed to go to Heaven. How long your soul spent in Purgatory was decided by God. But Hell was for eternity.

As my thoughts swung between the pros and cons of Purgatory and Hell, Sister Agatha watched me, eyes glinting with spite.

"Harmony Brown!" She shouted. "Are you listening to me?"

Keeping my head down, I jerked myself back from the abyss of my thoughts and nodded. Sister Agatha let go her grip on her rosary beads and gave me a sharp jab on my shoulder with her index finger.

"Well?"

"Yes, Sister." I glanced up at her face and quickly lowered my eyes. Her face was twisted and cruel, I loathed looking at her.

"God," she said, "is merciful." She paused looked around the class and turned back to me. "But you." She stopped and waited for her prediction of my fate to sink in. "You will go to Hell for rejecting the Catholic Church. You are a bold girl." Her words were said with such venom spittle formed at the corners of her mouth. When I didn't react, she continued. "God in his Mercy." She turned back to the class. "God in his Mercy has been gracious enough to make Harmony Brown a Catholic and has accepted her into the one true faith." She paused watching the faces of the children before her.

Then her voice rose punctuating the silence. "Harmony is a wicked girl who ought to be grateful and not shame God by saying she is going to leave the Catholic Church."

I hung my head until my chin touched my chest and wondered if Hell could be worse than this moment?

She leaned towards me. "Once a Catholic, always a Catholic," she said. "Do you understand?"

I noticed her lips had become an even thinner line, thin and cruel. Her threats made me more determined I would definitely not be a Catholic when I grew up. Perhaps, I thought, Purgatory or Hell had something going for them if it meant getting away from her.

She looked down her long thin nose watching me closely. "Being a Christian is not good enough. You have to be a Catholic to get into heaven, don't forget that, you wicked, bold girl?"

She gave a loud sniff and tapped the cane against the toe of her shoe. "You want to go to Heaven don't you?"

Could I say no? I thought of the possibility of asking her if she was going to be in Heaven too and if so, perhaps I would decline God's kind offer.

I had no choice. "Yes, Sister," I whispered.

"Yes Sister, what?" She barked, challenging me to disagree, her icy pale blue eyes holding mine.

I shivered. "Yes, Sister Agatha." I hung my head again. I didn't like her eyes and neither did I like the way she was staring at me. I felt as though I was on the edge of a precipice being edged backwards bit-by-bit towards a deep black crevice waiting to swallow me up. She was close, too close, and the cane was within striking distance. Getting enough air into my lungs was becoming increasingly difficult.

"Yes, Sister Agatha what?" She demanded, her voice shrill with impatience.

I wasn't sure what I was supposed to say, but I knew I had better come up with something quickly, so I made a wild guess.

"Yes, Sister Agatha. I want to go to Heaven."

"Right." She folded her arms across her chest, her voice resounded with pride at having made a convert. She breathed out satisfied as though she was in charge of giving out passes to Heaven and if I repented... if I begged hard enough... if I was subservient enough, if I knew my place, I might receive one from her.

I looked straight ahead avoiding her eyes.

She turned to the class. "Well children, God has decided to forgive Harmony Brown, she is a very lucky girl." She smiled, rather I think it was meant to be a smile, but her top lip folded completely into her mouth leaving a straight line with a fractional tilt at the corners.

It was a look I found quite unnerving, as it was the same look she'd had on her face when earlier she'd brought the cane forcefully down on the palm of my hand.

"Now Harmony Brown," she said turning back to me. "You have to say five Our Fathers, five Hail Marys and five Glory Be to the Father as penance and in thanksgiving for Our Lord Jesus Christ the Son of God forgiving you."

"Yes Sister," I whispered. Like hell, a little voice in my head said as my heart lifted rebelliously. Yet, I was getting confused. What happened to God? Now it seemed Jesus, the Son of God was forgiving me. When did he get into all of this? Wasn't God going to forgive me?

"And to make sure you do, you will come to my office at playtime and say them. Sister Martha Mary will make sure you don't forget."

She nodded to Sister Martha Mary, who throughout had been hovering anxiously beside the blackboard her eyes fixed on me, her lips tight, her expression fluctuating between anxiety and anger as though I had betrayed her. I was told to hang my coat up again and return to my seat.

My mother had once said we could think anything we wanted as long as we only said it silently to ourselves. Generations of *coloured* people survived in the face of all the iniquities handed down throughout history by using such a strategy, she'd said. Remember, she'd emphasised, "no one can stop you from thinking anything you want to think as long as you don't turn those thoughts into words."

I was only eight, and as Sister Agatha was ranting shrilly before me, I tightened my lips and kept my thoughts to myself. My parents had often lamented I had a bad habit of saying what came into my mind without any thought of the consequences. Not true, on this occasion I kept my lips tightly held together.

"And stop grimacing like a monkey." Sister Agatha snarled her lips pulled back against her teeth. As she spat the words at me, eyes glinting in undisguised fury, her fingers tightened once more, on the cane.

I wasn't sure what she meant. Grimacing? Did she mean grinning? Only I wasn't grinning and how she thought I looked like a monkey, I couldn't fathom.

I lowered my head further as shame washed over me and I became even more conscious of the eyes of the entire class on me. Did they think I looked like as monkey too? I was mortified. Heat flooded my entire body and I was thankful I was *coloured* because they wouldn't notice if I went red.

Why, why, why? I asked myself as despair engulfed me, did she think I looked like a monkey? It was then I remembered, monkeys weren't Catholics...didn't have to be. I lifted my head and looked into a face registering loathing. I longed to tell her monkeys didn't have to be Catholics. But being *bold* was one thing, being called a monkey quite another, but then again, being stupid was totally different and I wasn't stupid particularly as I was aware of the cane still gripped tightly in her hand and the chilblains on my fingers swollen, itching painfully and now bleeding.

Sister Agatha had said I looked like a monkey in front of my class and everyone had heard her. I had to bite down hard on the inside of my lip to stop it wobbling as I looked up at the face of a Bride of Christ suffused with hatred. And so at the tender age of eight, I knew without a doubt, not only what hate looked like, but what hate felt like too.

CHAPTER 6

The only consolation of my having to spend playtime in Sister Agatha's office, was that her office was warm. It was far better than having to spend fifteen minutes in the cold dreary playground.

And so, when the bell announced playtime, Sister Martha Mary reminded me of my penance and I skipped down to Sister Agatha's office with alacrity. Saying a few prayers wouldn't be so bad and I would be warm.

I arrived at Sister Agatha's office knocked, told to come in and kneel. But just as I was settling down to say my penance with hands folded in prayer and my eyes focused on the statue of the Virgin Mary set on a small table covered with a white lace cloth, I heard Bridget Flannigan outside in the playground organizing the game of the Princess and the Wicked Witch.

"Harmony isn't here, so you can be the Wicked Witch, Bernadette."

"No." Bernadette squealed in her high voice. "It's not fair, you're always the Princess and I'm always the maid and now I'm supposed to be the Wicked Witch. I'm not playing."

"Okay, we will pick for it."

Bernadette was appeased, and I heard them deciding who would be the Wicked Witch, though I knew Bridget would be the Princess regardless.

"Eeni meenni minni mo, catch a nigger by his toe. If he hollas let him go. Eeni meenni minni mo. O.U.T spells out."

"Harmony Brown you're here to say your penance, not daydream," Sister Agatha snapped behind me. 'I want to hear you praying for forgiveness."

I quickly made the sign of the cross and almost wished I were outside playing with Bridget and Bernadette, even if I had to be the witch again. But then again, it was warm in here.

I spent the next fifteen minutes on my knees in front of a small statue of the Virgin Mary. She was blond, pink-cheeked, blue-eyed and decked out in a lovely blue satin cape over a white satin robe.

I prayed slowly hoping I would be able to spin out my penance until the end of playtime. I was aware of Sister Agatha seated behind me sipping a cup of tea delivered from the staffroom, by a *favourite*. At least, I consoled myself, I wasn't on the cold playground and neither was I being caned.

In between sips of tea and nibbling on a biscuit, Sister Agatha watched me. "Speak up Harmony, I'm sure God wants to hear you," she said sharply at one point.

I raised my voice. "Glory be to the Father and to the Son and to the Holy Ghost Amen," I intoned loudly as the bell announcing the end of play rang out. Her cup clinked on the saucer.

"You may go."

"Thank you, Sister Agatha." I stood and slipped out the door to join my class.

Of course, it was inevitable Sister Agatha, and I would cross paths several times on my journey through her school. She appeared to be on a mission to make sure all the evil she saw in me was eradicated, and that my classmates knew the danger I posed to their entry into heaven, should they get caught up in any of my boldness.

Being *coloured* was a sin in Sister Agatha eyes, one I was somehow responsible for and it was her mission to make sure I paid the price. Given any opportunity she would add the cane to stress how fortunate I was to be one of the saved despite the colour of my skin.

She wanted me to be grateful for being accepted into her school and the Catholic Church. She wanted me to come to terms with my unfortunate condition. But in her eyes, I persisted in being unrepentant...being frequently a bold wicked girl and always a picannini bordering on the brink of paganism.

CHAPTER 7

Sister Cuthbert, our teacher the following year, also wielded her power through the cane, without which she appeared weak and spineless.

She too found me unnerving and would ignore me most of the time, which I liked. Though I didn't learn to read and left at the end of the year with a report placing me thirty-ninth out of forty, I didn't mind. I wasn't last. Francis Doyle was fortieth. She was always last.

Francis Doyle was the girl with dirty limp hair, threadbare summer dresses and thin cardigans even in the middle of winter. She continually sported two goblets of green snot hanging precariously over her top lip during both winter and summer and all the months between.

I once sat opposite her during lunch and saw, to my horror, one of the goblets of green fall onto her watery mashed potato. It happened just as I was about to put a forkful of green slimy over-cooked cabbage in my mouth.

I still retch at the memory of Francis Doyle clearing her plate and wonder how I managed to hold down the contents of my stomach. But it was fear...fear, a strong motivator as I had once seen Sister

Agatha forcing a crying five-year-old on her first day at school, to eat her own vomit.

It was in Sister Cuthbert's class, during one of our music and movement lessons that I was first called immodest.

We were asked to dance to the beat of the drum Sister Cuthbert banged unenthusiastically as we all pranced barefooted around the hall. We girls were in our navy blue serge bloomers and white vests, and the boys in...to be honest, I can't remember, must have been shorts...and vests. The boys wore grey short trousers, even in the middle of winter.

The hall also served as our dining-hall and still contained not only the smell of over-boiled cabbage and mince stew, but also remnants of cold mashed potato squelching beneath our feet and between our toes, as we danced.

We were instructed by Sister Cuthbert to move to the beat of her drumming, fast, slow, fast, fast, slow. We did as we were told. The boys leapt and jumped like wild uninhibited *jungle people,* as Sister Cuthbert called their efforts. She praised them for their enthusiasm. The girls pointed their toes and twirled in an effort to be dainty ballerinas.

I wiggled my bottom in an effort to dance in time to the beat, though difficult because Sister Cuthbert had little idea of rhythm. As I danced, I became increasingly aware of Sister Cuthbert watching me dance. Her eyes followed me around the room as she urged the class on.

At first, I thought she liked my efforts since I moved with more of a sense of rhythm than the others around me. She stopped banging the drum, made everyone sit down cross-legged and turned to me.

"Come here Harmony," she said. Her lips took on the same disappearing act as Sister Agatha's mean thin crack of a mouth and I knew instinctively, I had done something wrong.

"I think your dance is inappropriate, child."

"Yes, Sister," I replied not sure what she meant. Did she mean she liked it? Perhaps she did like my efforts to dance.

I smiled happily. It was rare Sister Cuthbert spoke to me directly, so to have her stop everyone, make them sit down and say something nice to me, made my heart lift.

She saw my pleasure at her words and her voice took on a sharpness that should have warned me, she was not pleased.

"Your dance is immodest."

Immodest! What did she mean? What had I done? The smile fell away from my lips as I turned my large eyes towards her.

Immodest? Immodest was a sin we were told to confess when we went to confession every week. I never knew what it meant, but made sure to tell the priest every week, I had been immodest. We had to confess, not only our actions but also our words and thoughts. With each sin confessed, we had to say whether it was a word, thought or deed.

My confessions usually amounted to the following, "Bless me, Father, for I have sinned. It has been a week since my last confession. I was unkind in word, I told a lie, and I was immodest in my thoughts." I believed I had covered it all. Sometimes I would change the sins around just to make it look as though I had given thought to my sins and truly wanted forgiveness. One week I may be immodest in thought, the next, in words and the following week in deeds. I'm only thankful Father Kelly never asked me to clarify what it was I had done to be immodest, as I wouldn't have known what to say.

But here I was being called immodest. Immodest, I surmised, must be something to do with dancing.

Sister Cuthbert must have seen the bewilderment on my face and gave a small, no lip smile then added in a vague way. "I think it would be better if you came and did the drumming like they do in Africa where you come from."

I opened my mouth to tell her I didn't come from Africa, that I was born in England, in Coventry, to be precise.

But not wanting to disappoint her, I said nothing. Something inside me recognised she may be trying to be kind. So, I took her place at the drum and beat it in frenzy, as I imagined black people did in Africa.

More wild dancing and leaping around from the boys followed

and the girls, continued to tiptoe, pointing their toes and twirling around, however I drummed.

On another occasion, again during a Physical Education lesson, in the same, after lunch watery mashed potato carpeted hall, Sister Cuthbert told us to walk around the hall balancing small rubber rings on our heads.

"Stop," she called and we all stood still. She looked at me, her eyes withering to pinpricks. "Harmony Brown, come here."

My heart sank. Had I been immodest again? What had I done?

"I want you all to watch Harmony, she knows how to do it. In Africa where Harmony comes from, people carry things on their heads all the time."

All eyes turned to me as I was told to walk around the hall with a rubber ring balanced on my head to show everyone how to do it. I felt desperately awkward and afraid she would find fault. I liked being praised for doing something right, but I could never be sure with Sister Cuthbert.

I started slowly at first and when she said no more, I walked with more confidence knowing everyone's eyes were on me. It felt good, really good, to be doing something right for a change.

I found it easy to keep the rubber ring on my head because my hair was thick and frizzy, not thin and slippery like the others. In truth, the rubber ring would have had to have, a life of its own to slip off my hair, no matter how I walked.

"Look how straight she holds her back," Sister Cuthbert pointed out after my third round of the hall. "Look at her neck, see how tall and straight she holds it."

She smiled like Sister Agatha, again no lips, as though a particularly bad smell had just passed her way and something inside me shivered ominously.

CHAPTER 8

I was buoyant with the praise I received from Sister Cuthbert and when we returned to class, she stood and watched as we dressed, urging us to hurry. I wanted her continuing praise, I wanted her to like me, so did as ordered. When dressed I slid onto my seat crossed my arms and sat up straight.

"Harmony," she said when we girls had slipped into our skirts and the boys into their shirts. "Come out to the front and tell us what it was like living in Africa." She appeared to be determined to make the most of my *Africaness*.

I quaked with fear. I'd been had taken to Africa when I was two years old to visit my mother's relatives, but we hadn't stayed long enough to call it home and my mother had always talked of England as home.

What was I supposed to say? I couldn't remember very much.

"It was...it was very hot," I stammered looking longingly towards the large iron stove in the corner of the room where Sister Cuthbert's desk was placed. She must have some idea of what hot was like as I often caught her standing very close to the fire during the winter blocking the heat from the rest of us.

"And what else, child?" She asked from her corner seat next to the stove.

My mind swung back to the conundrum of what Africa was like...yes, Africa was hot, but what else?

"Yes, hot." Sister Cuthbert repeated nodding her head in agreement and urging me on. "Did you live in the jungle?"

"Yes." I nodded. In fact, I wasn't sure what she meant by jungle. I don't think I ever saw a jungle. We had lived in a town where there were a few trees, lots of people and houses. The roads between towns had scatterings of huts and trees interspersed with grass-lands, generally referred to as *the bush*. No one I knew lived in a jungle.

She looked at me expectantly. If she believed everyone in Africa lived in a jungle, I loathed the idea of disappointing her. She'd been nice to me, and I wanted her to go on being nice to me. I desperately wanted her to like me.

"There were lots of trees...big trees." It sounded lame, and the words died on my lips. I looked around helplessly for inspiration. I looked longingly towards my desk.

"Were there any wild animals in your village?" She was determined not to let me off the hook. Jungle, village, wild animals? What next? So now I lived in a village? Perhaps she thought I lived in a village in a jungle?

I nodded racking my brain desperately trying to think of animals I'd seen at Regents Park Zoo the previous summer, those my parents had pointed out as having come from Africa. I certainly hadn't seen them when I was in Africa.

"Well, child, tell us." Sister Cuthbert pressed. Her hands tapped impatiently on the desk in front of her and my mind raced, desper-ately searching for something that would satisfy her need to make me truly African.

Monkeys came to mind, but then I remembered being likened to a monkey by Sister Agatha, so thought it unwise to mention them.

In desperation, I blurted out, "Tigers."

Sister Cuthbert looked momentarily puzzled. "Tigers?" she

murmured and then nodded a fleeting look of satisfaction etched on her face. "Good."

I sighed with relief, my ordeal was over, I knew tigers didn't come from Africa, but it seemed, she didn't.

She turned to the class checking no one was messing around and after a sharp rebuke to Gerry McNamara to stop playing with the inkwell, turned back to me. My heart sank.

"Tell us about the hut you lived in Harmony."

Hut? I must have looked puzzled because in reality I had lived in a bungalow and we'd had a large garden, a gardener and a cook and also someone to look after me while my mother worked. And now I lived in a small flat in North London and before our flat, we had lived in rooms, sharing a kitchen and toilet with other tenants somewhere in Paddington. What was I going to say about living in a hut in Africa?

Then mercifully I remembered the story of the Three Little Pigs, and I gave an inward sigh of relief. "Our hut was made out of straw," I said loudly holding my head high and smiled pleased with my ingenuity.

"Just straw?" It was Sister Cuthbert's turn to look confused. "Surely, something else as well?"

"Yes." My mind desperately searched for what else.

"Mud?" She suggested helpfully.

"Yes Sister," I agreed almost joyously. "Straw and mud."

She nodded.

Thankful my ordeal was truly over, I prepared to make my way back to my desk.

"Has anyone got any questions to ask Harmony about living in a mud hut in the jungle in Africa?" She asked, dragging out the impromptu geography lesson.

My heart sank again. What did I know about mud huts? What did I know about Africa?

One hand shot up. Patrick O'Shea. It just had to be him. I shuddered. For some reason, I couldn't fathom, he hated me, and so in return, I hated him in equal measure. He was always trying to hurt me either pinching me if he thought no one was looking, pulling my plaits or hissing *'blackie, blackie'* in a low voice if ever we were near each other.

All the teachers liked Patrick, especially Sister Agatha who was always holding him up as a good example. Patrick was a paragon of virtue, according to Sister Agatha. He came from a large Catholic family, and his father was also a Catholic.

Sister Agatha frequently reminded me that my father wasn't a Catholic, as though it was a great failing on my part. But it wasn't from lack of trying, my mother and I said the rosary every night in an effort to beg The Virgin Mary, to convert my father, so he could go to heaven.

But now, I was facing Patrick O'Shea as he stood with an evil smile on his face. He was very clever, he could read, which I couldn't and to top it all, he was an altar boy so would be excused lessons on Friday afternoon to go up to the church and prepare for Benediction.

"Yes, Patrick," Sister Cuthbert said her voice softening. "Would you like to ask Harmony a question about living in a mud hut in Africa?"

"Yes, Sister," Patrick replied politely. Looking at him standing behind his desk, he looked angelic and it was difficult to imagine he'd always shouted rude things to me as I walked down the road from school on the way home. One of his favourite barbs was, "Go home to where you come from monkey face."

Now, as he stood cherub-like, pink-cheeked, looking at me, a spiteful look in his eyes, I knew he was going to try to humiliate me. I shook with fear, preparing for his question. I was determined he wouldn't see how he made me feel, and I held my head high, my shoulders back and waited.

Sister Cuthbert smiled at him. "Good boy Patrick." She turned to the class. "I hope you all listen to what Patrick is going to say."

Patrick telling me to go home to where I came from, always baffled me as I was already home, besides he had not long come from Ireland. But now under the adoring eyes of Sister Cuthbert, he looked at me, his blue eyes glinting with satisfaction, a mean smile curving his lips, enjoying my fear as I stood in front of the class, at his mercy.

Apprehensive I gripped my hands tightly together in front of me, feeling hot and cold in turn.

"Did you get wet in your hut when it rained?" He stared hard at me, daring me to answer.

He knows I'm lying, I thought. I hate him. I hate him. The unspoken words resounded around and around in my head. I held my head up proudly and looked directly at him, into those mean pale blue eyes and vowed I would never let him see how frightened he made me feel.

"Sometimes." My voice gathered strength as I looked at him, looked at his cruel smile. "If it rained very hard, some of it would come in." It made sense to me. Of course, the rain must get in sometimes, after all, it only took a few puffs from the big bad wolf to blow the little pig's house down. Surely straw and a little bit of mud wouldn't be very weather-proof?

"Well, there we are then," Sister Cuthbert interrupted, looking relieved as the bell announcing playtime rang. "We've all learned something about Africa today. Thank you, Patrick."

Her charitable deed for the day ticked off she could retreat to the staffroom with the knowledge her place in Heaven was assured.

At the end of the day, as we all stood, placed our chairs on our desks and folded our hands for night prayers, I closed my eyes tightly. The Act of Contrition was intoned, "Bless me, Father, for I have sinned..." I prayed to God to forgive me for all the sins I had committed, particularly for all the lies I had told about living in Africa.

I prayed extra hard God would understand and forgive me. I really didn't want to go to Hell.

CHAPTER 9

By the time I was ten, I'd lost all illusion life was fair. I no longer held out any hope Sister Agatha would ignore me and stop accusing me of being evil, if I tried to be less bold. I'd long given up any belief she would stop caning me for every imagined transgression.

I often didn't know what I'd done to deserve her ire. I asked myself often, what would I have to do to become a good girl? I had long decided, being ignored by Sister Agatha would be true Heaven.

It was then, during my penultimate year at school with Sister Agatha still watching my every move that we clashed for the last time.

It had been a wonderful summer, a long hot summer holiday, idyllic. It was a summer filled

with glorious hot days followed by long warm light summer evenings.

I'd stayed with my cousins in Liverpool for the summer, and we'd been free to roam returning home only for meals and bed. It was the summer I saw, *I love Lucy* on television for the first time. I loved playing with my cousins, exploring the woods and playing in the street with other children.

My mother had instructed me not to miss Mass. Missing Sunday Mass, she reminded me was a mortal sin, the greatest sin in the world. I remembered Sister Agatha saying, a mortal sin was even worse than being a heathen as it would be a one-way ticket to Hell.

My Aunt arranged for a Catholic family living two doors down, to take me to Mass each Sunday. We played with their children during those long hot summer days and when their parents were at work, they would take us into their parents' bedroom to see the spare wooden leg, their father kept under the bed. He had lost a leg during the Second World War and in 1954 the war was still close enough for many families to be living with its aftermath.

Much of our day as spent in the street playing hopscotch, chase and hide and seek. I don't remember it raining once, though it must have done. Through those long hot summer days, I wasn't called *Blackie* once. Can you imagine how wonderful it was? If anything was Heaven, my holiday with my cousins certainly was. It was a time of total happiness and I never once thought of school, the times-tables, Catechism or Sister Agatha.

But September came and I returned home to London. School loomed, a black cloud on the horizon of what had been a perfect summer and I feared what lay ahead. Another year of the cane was a certainty.

~

The morning school started, I found we had a new teacher, Mr O'Neal. He appeared friendly and I considered myself luckier than my friends in the class above whose teacher was the dreaded Mr Nolan who so loved his cane and was never to be seen without it. I say *it*, but I should say *them*, for he had several.

As I walked home from school on the first day of term, my friend recounted how Mr Nolan had greeted his new class.

He'd introduced himself and then introduced his best friends. "I want you all to meet my best friends," he'd said and turning to a tall cupboard behind his desk he'd thrown open the doors. "These are my best friends."

Hanging on pegs in neat rows, were different size canes both in length and in thickness. They were displayed on specially devised pegs to enable him to retrieve one easily and quickly. As he'd spoken he'd run his fingers lovingly along them as though playing a stringed instrument. I felt sad for my friend and was glad our new teacher was so nice.

Mr O'Neil was my first male teacher. He smiled at us a lot on our first day together and there was no cane in sight. He smiled more than any teacher I had ever known and he didn't have a cane perpetually on his desk. He actually seemed to like us.

Every teacher had a daily routine of lining us around the class-room wall. *"Five sevens? Four twos? Three sevens?"* they'd shout pointing their cane at each of us in turn, and we'd be told to hold our hands out and receive a whack of the cane if we hesitated or didn't answer fast enough. I was so terrified at what awaited me each morning, I wet the bed every night.

Mr O'Neal didn't cane us for not knowing our tables, nor did he brandish the cane when during the next half of the morning, we had to answer Catechism questions.

It was the first time in my school life I didn't get the cane on a daily basis for not knowing my Times-Tables or Catechism. My life normally filled with fear started to change in Mr O'Neal's class. God began to appear almost benevolent. The fear of constant punishment faded, and I was happy.

CHAPTER 10

I 'd seen Mr O'Neal before he became our teacher. I thought then he was nice and very good-looking. He was young and all the other teachers were old. I hadn't known, when Sister Agatha brought him into our classroom at the end of the summer term, he would be our new teacher.

As Sister Agatha stood before us, her visitor beside her, I prayed to the Virgin Mary to protect me from her, even if it meant I had to die.

Being in the vicinity of Sister Agatha was perilous and always spelt the likelihood of physical danger. She would inevitably look for a way to humiliate me and point out any failing she saw in me, and then use the cane to emphasise my faults. I was right to fear her because on this occasion, I didn't have long to wait.

We all rose to our feet as we had been instructed to do each time a grown-up entered the classroom and trot out our greeting be it, morning or afternoon.

"Sit down, children," she said as she moved into the room. "Well now." She showed her teeth, a rare occurrence. With Sister Agatha, any resemblance to a smile was usually a tight slash across her face with a hint of an upturn at the corner of her lips.

"Who can answer this question?"

One girl had already raised her hand even before the question was asked.

"Francis Doyle put your hand down and wait for the question," Sister Agatha snapped. Francis hung her head dejectedly and sniffed.

Mary Murphy sat straight-backed, arms folded in front of her, cheeks pink with excitement as she waited for the question.

"Who made you?" Sister Agatha's voice rang out.

Mary's hand shot up as though she was reaching for the sky. Other hands waved wildly in the air.

"Mary," Sister Agatha said pointing the cane she'd been carrying concealed in her skirt. "You seem to be the only one who is sitting up properly. You can tell us."

I sighed with relief, the stiffness in my spine softened and I sat back in my seat. I'd escaped. I would be safe and forgotten. Mary would give the correct answer, she always did and Sister Agatha would be pleased and go away.

Mary stood slowly and gracefully. Sister Agatha nodded her head encouragingly.

"God made us." Mary's reply rang out clearly and loudly, her voice resonating around the classroom.

"Good girl Mary. Sit down, child."

Turning to the man standing at her side Sister Agatha whispered loudly. "Mary is one of our best pupils. Her family comes from County Cork."

He nodded.

"Is that right child?"

Mary stood again. "Yes, Sister."

"A good Catholic family," Sister Agatha said and nodded as Mary sat.

"Now," she turned back to the class. Her eyes oscillated around the rows of children with a purpose and finally settled on me. "Stand up Harmony."

I trembled as I stood feeling the blood drain from my face. The Saints hadn't protected me, I had been let down in my moment of dire need.

"Harmony comes from Africa," she said to the man and turned back to pierce me with a look of distaste.

"In whose image did God make you?" She barked as she emphasised the word *you*. Her lips tightened with dislike and her eyes flashed with annoyance.

I opened my mouth, no words emerged, and I could not remember whose image God made me. For a start I didn't look a bit like God, he was white, with blue eyes and blond hair. I know because each class had a picture of him. I knew Sister Agatha had asked me the question, so she could torture me because she thought I looked like a monkey. I bit my lip and looked down.

"Everyone here could answer that question Harmony." She swept the cane in an arc around the class. "Don't you dare stand there saying nothing Harmony Brown."

I stood motionless waiting for the inevitable cane.

"Answer me," Sister Agatha demanded and her voice rose shrilly as she advanced towards me. "Answer me or come and get the cane."

"God made me in..." I stopped, I couldn't remember. Fear of the inevitable had robbed me of words, memory and the ability to move. The man was staring at me curiously. He didn't look angry like Sister Agatha.

The class was silent, each child grateful they weren't the focus of Sister Agatha's attention. Humiliation swamped me. I tugged at one of my plaits nervously, and the ribbon came away in my hand.

"Leave your hair alone," Sister Agatha shouted. "You are a vain, bold girl who should pay more attention to being a good Catholic, not on how you look."

She came to stand in front of me, her eyes wild with rage and snatched the ribbon from my hand, dropped it on the floor and stamped on it. "Vanity," she hissed as she towered over me. "Are you not going to answer the question?"

I shrank back and silently stuck out my hand, palm up and bit down hard on my bottom lip as the cane swished down and connected with my flesh.

I tasted blood in my mouth and my eyes watered, but I refused to cry out. Lowering my eyes, I focused hard on Sister Agatha's shiny black leather laced shoes. I had to concentrate, so I wouldn't cry out, so she wouldn't see how much she'd hurt me.

The shoes turned and walked away, black skirt trailing behind. It had ended, my torturer was walking away... the black shoes were walking away, the long black skirt flapping against low stacked heels heralded my reprieve, my torturer was leaving. I let out a shaky breath and slid down onto my seat. Sister Agatha would leave me alone now.

"You see what I mean Mr O'Neal, we must all pray for the missionaries in Africa." She swung round at the head of the class and turned towards Mary. "Mary, you tell us, child," she said her voice softening.

Mary stood again, a faint blush reddening her cheeks and brushed a strand of blond hair back from her face.

"God made us in his image and likeness to love him...honour him and obey in this world and..."

The rest of the words were lost as I focused on Mary's pink lips, pale skin and dusting of pink on her cheeks. I wondered what it would be like to look like Mary, to be white, to have blond hair and blue eyes. And I wondered what it would feel like to be liked by Sister Agatha and all the teachers?

If I had straight blond hair and pink cheeks, would I be popular like Mary? Would I always be asked to join in games without ever having to ask? Would I get to take messages to different classes when our teacher needed something? Would I get to be the leader of a team in the PE lessons? Would I be first in the line going out to play? I couldn't imagine it.

"Good girl Mary." Sister Agatha nodded at Mary, turned towards the door and beckoned Mr O'Neal to follow her.

"Thank you, Sister Cuthbert," she said as she reached the door. "Because of Mary the class can go out to play a few minutes early... except for Harmony Brown, she can stay behind and learn her Catechism."

The fact, I couldn't read and therefore would be sitting staring at the red Catechism book throughout playtime, didn't matter.

Sister Cuthbert nodded. "Thank you, Sister Agatha." She turned to glare at me as though I had let her down.

"And Mary you can come down to my office later, I may have a sweet for you." Sister Agatha swung round and strode purposely through the door with Mr O'Neal trailing close behind.

"Matthew Keegan," Sister Cuthbert said. "Choose someone and go and bring the milk crate in." She smiled. "And Vivian, give out the straws."

I watched as Vivian sprang to her feet and collected the box of straws from the cupboard, her short dark straight hair swinging just below her ears. She turned and started down the rows of desks carefully dispensing straws.

I longed for straight hair. I wanted straight hair, floppy straight hair. Most of all as I watched Vivian giving out the straws, I longed to be trusted to do such an important job as giving out the straws.

Vivian looked down when she reached me and dropped a straw on my desk. "You can't play with us at playtime. *You* have to stay in," she hissed.

She moved on to the next desk.

CHAPTER 11

Mr O'Neal was very different from the rest of the teachers. He rarely used the cane, instead, he built an alliance with us. If Sister Agatha appeared suddenly, prowling around like a large angry panther, he would hear her squeaky shoes and reach for his cane looking at us sternly and she would nod approvingly through the glass in the door and move on to the next class. He would then put the cane down and smile at us. He was our friend, and we liked and trusted him.

School became a place I began to enjoy even though Mr O'Neal didn't let us sit with our friends. Boys and girls were separated, and we girls had to sit next to a boy. Mr O'Neal said it was because there was too much chattering going on.

I liked Mr O'Neal, so forgave him for placing me next to a boy, besides I was lucky, the boy I sat next to was James Baxter. He was nice to me and told me he liked my eyes because they were like his best brown marbles.

"Your eyes are like my marbles," he whispered one day as we came in from play. "They're beautiful."

He always picked me as his partner in our country dancing lessons and he never pulled my plaits or called me names.

I basked in his compliments and fell in love with him right away. No one had ever said anything nice about how I looked. I never forgot him.

As a class, we learned very quickly Mr O'Neal had certain rules and only when those rules were breached in any way, would he get angry. On those occasions, we would sit, quaking with fear at what we may have unleashed. When he got angry, his blue eyes would turn chilly like the sky before snow. His mouth would form a tight straight line, and something in his cheek would twitch as his chin set. Worst of all, his hands would fist and unfist as he stood before us, as though he was holding himself in check.

A frisson of fear would ripple through the class. One angry look alone would make the naughtiest boy in the class, Brian Davies, stop in his tracks and tremble. It was strange the effect Mr O'Neal's suppressed anger had on us. He rarely used the cane, and usually only if Sister Agatha was in the vicinity or had instructed him to cane someone.

We learned Mr O'Neal was newly married, and his wife was expecting a baby in April, the same time as my mother. Such information shared with us was unusual in itself because none of the teachers told us anything personal about themselves. I was happy, because Mr O'Neal and I shared something special.

Mr O'Neal rarely left the vicinity of his desk. He wouldn't walk around the class smacking the cane against his trouser leg as a reminder of what was to come. If he moved from his desk at all, it would be only to the blackboard behind him. We felt safe.

"When you come up to get your books marked," he said one morning after being unusually active with his angry looks and to our horror, the cane. "The boys must line up on my right and the girls on my left side."

I went up to get my sums marked, and Mr O'Neal started to pat me on my bottom with his left hand. When he had finished marking my work, most of it with red crosses, he told me I was a good girl. I found it a little puzzling, but who was I to complain? I told, I was a good girl.

I skipped happily back to my seat and proceeded to complete more sums even though each time I returned to Mr O'Neal, I received more crosses than ticks. Despite all the crosses he gave me, he continued to pat my bottom with his left hand and tell me I was a good girl. From then on, after each marking session, he told me I was a good girl as he patted my bottom some more. He was right-handed, in case you're wondering.

It was a relief when Mr O'Neal didn't seem to mind my errors, he didn't shout at me as he did with the boys. He spent some brief time helping me understand my mistakes, all the while he kept his hand on my bottom patting it over my skirt. I found it difficult to concentrate on what he was saying and so my knowledge of mathematical concepts failed to improve.

One morning, Mr O'Neal told me to stand closer when he was marking my book and what followed was to change my life forever.

I had begun to stand out of his hand-patting reach since it had started to feel a bit too much. One or two pats I could accept, but a continual pat, pat, pat the whole time I stood next to him was too much. It was too uncomfortable, too awkward, and somehow it didn't feel quite right. I couldn't put my finger on it, but I began to hate going to get my books marked, even though he told me each time I was a good girl.

"You can't see how I'm working out this sum for you..." he told me. "...If you stand so far away."

The tone of his voice sounded angry and nasty, and for the first time, I was frightened of Mr O'Neal.

Reluctantly I moved a little closer and just before he sent me back to my desk, he put his hand up my skirt, and this time patted me on my bottom over my navy-blue knickers.

"Good girl," he said and sent me back to my desk before he called a boy to come up and get his book marked. The boy stood at Mr O'Neil's right-hand side. I saw he kept his left hand for us, girls.

CHAPTER 12

I crept back to my desk and as I slid onto my seat I looked around at the other girls. They didn't seem worried and they all appeared absorbed in their work. The class was quiet except for Mr O'Neal's voice as he called out a girl and then a boy.

When the girls were at his desk, no one was allowed to disturb him, either by putting up their hand or coming up to his desk. If anyone disturbed him, he would shout at them.

I avoided finishing my work hoping Mr O'Neal would just send me back to my desk. Each day he would make sure to call me up, even though I hadn't finished my work.

"Harmony," he called one morning. "Come and get your book marked."

He sounded stern and I was worried he was going to be angry with me. I trembled and a growing feeling of fear slid through me as I made my way to his desk and stood on his left.

If only Mr O'Neal would stop touching me under my skirt, life would be perfect. I didn't like it but how could I make it stop without him getting angry with me?

"Harmony," he said softly when I reached him and placed my book open at the unfinished page of sums, before him.

"Don't you like coming up to get your books marked anymore?"

I hung my head and said nothing as shame at what I knew he would do next engulfed me. He'd moved from patting to stroking. He slipped his hand up my skirt and started stroking, no longer patting my bottom over my navy-blue knickers.

"Do you like me helping you get your sums right?" he said softly.

I nodded.

"Well then," he said his voice low, "if you like it, you should come up without me having to get angry with you." His hand slipped between my legs gently pushing my thighs apart and started stroking the inside of my thighs. It was such an unfamiliar experience my thighs quivered.

"There," he said softly. "I know you like me helping you. Say it. Say you like me helping you."

"Yes, Sir," I croaked as heat flooded me. I felt ashamed, I was frightened, I felt sick, it was a hundred times worse than school dinners.

"Say it, Harmony, say you like it." His voice was silky soft with an edge of a threat.

I was frightened.

Almost gagging and swallowing the bile rising in my throat, I whispered the words he wanted to hear.

"Yes, Sir, I like it,"

"Good," he said satisfied and pulled my book closer. " Now I want to show you how to do this sum."

Tears welled up in my eyes and I held my breath.

"When you do, a division sum always make sure..."

His words were lost in the drumming of blood in my ears. I wanted to die. I knew it shouldn't be happening, but what would happen if I asked him to stop. He would blame me, say I wanted him to do it, say I liked it and I would get into trouble, without a doubt, I would get the cane and be sent to Sister Agatha.

His hand moved, his pulled at the elastic of my knicker-leg and let it snap gently back onto my thigh.

I went ridged. He continued stroking my thigh and then for the first time put his hand right inside my knickers and started to stroke me there...yes there, my foo-foo, as we called it. He touched me there where no one touched, not even me when I bathed because we weren't supposed to.

I had never had any of those strange feelings before, and I gasped and tried to pull away. His hand held me fast and when I was still, he slipped his hand out of my knickers and stroked my thigh again.

"You see, it's good when I help you with your work," he said quietly and patted my bottom.

"Am I good to you?"

"Yes, Sir," I whispered as I picked up my book. I felt dizzy with horror and shame. Was it my fault he had done those things to me?

"Make sure to come up to my desk every day to get your work marked. I don't want to have to get angry with you again."

I nodded.

"Be a good girl. Go back and finish your sums."

It didn't feel right. It was horrible. I didn't know what to do. I wanted to be a good girl. I didn't want Mr O'Neal to be angry with me. I wanted Mr O'Neal to like me and not to cane me.

Perhaps men teachers would touch girls in their private place if they liked them and Mr O'Neal had been kind to me before all this. But just the same, I squirmed uncomfortably as I sat down. I didn't like it. I really, really, didn't like what he had done.

Was I the only girl whose bottom he touched? Vivian went up next, and I pretended to be doing my work but secretly I was watching what Mr O'Neal did. I saw his hand stroke Vivian's leg and disappear up her skirt.

You've no idea what a relief it was. I wasn't the only one. It must be all right then. Nobody seemed to be worried about it, the other girls hadn't said anything, perhaps they were all used to it happening.

Three more girls went up before break and each time I saw his hand go up their skirt. When they returned to their desks, they dropped their eyes to their book and didn't look at anyone. I watched, so I knew. No one spoke about what Mr O'Neal did to them and I began to wonder if I was the only one who didn't like it.

After the break, Francis Doyle was the last girl to go up before lunch and I noticed Mr O'Neal, didn't put his hand up her skirt. Perhaps, it was all right for men teachers to touch you under your skirt if they liked you and Mr O'Neal didn't like Francis. Who did? She was smelly and her nose stuff...ugh.

But try as I might, I still didn't like Mr O'Neal putting his hand up my skirt and into my knickers. I shuddered at the mere thought of it.

Perhaps there was something wrong with me?

CHAPTER 13

It was a Friday and I always looked forward to the weekend, now even more so. Mr O'Neal had begun to frighten me. I wanted him to stop putting his hand into my knickers and touching me there.

I tried hard to avoid going up to get my book marked. I wished he would be like the other teachers, mean and in love with his cane. Being caned was a hundred times preferable to having Mr O'Neal's hand inside my knickers.

Friday meant two days without having to worry about what Mr O'Neal was doing or going to do next. Being home felt safe.

The boy next door and I had our own secret club. We were planning to finish building a hideout at the bottom of his garden. I could hardly wait. We would pretend to spy on people going up the hill in case they were spies. I loved those games.

We sometimes made a cone out of paper, filled it with salt and chased birds around the garden. We believed, if we got close enough to a bird and tipped salt on its tail, it wouldn't be able to fly away, and we could make it a pet.

To be honest, I didn't want a bird as a pet but felt I had to join in and try to catch one. I hated the idea of a bird as a pet and worried if David knew, he might not want to play with me. Luckily we never managed to get close enough to any bird.

My mother's tummy was getting bigger and bigger. She had been told she had to spend as much time as possible resting with her feet up. The Doctor had said her blood pressure was too high. She had something called toxaemia and if she didn't rest they would have to take her into hospital.

At the weekend, when I wasn't chasing birds or spying on people walking up and down the road, I sat at the bottom of her bed.

"Are you going to get better?" I asked.

She smiled. "Of course. I just have to make sure and do what the doctor tells me."

Friday evenings were my most favourite time of the week. It was the night I didn't have to bathe, it was called, *dirty night*. All I had to do was wash my face, hands and quickly between my legs. The latter was only rapidly washed since I feared committing a mortal sin if I lingered too long in that region.

After my boiled egg and bread and butter supper, I would clean my teeth, put on my father's old vest and climb into bed beside my mother. I would sit up in bed next to her and listen as she read the next chapter from *Seven years in Tibet*. I loved the story and longed one day to travel to exciting places like the men in the book. I shuffled closer cuddling into her. I loved our special time together.

Sometimes she would buy me a *Dandy* or *Beano* comic and treat herself to a *Woman's Own* magazine. We'd sit in bed next to each other, luxuriating in the cosiness of being together.

But that evening, I couldn't stop thinking about what Mr O'Neal had said and done and I got more and more unhappy as the evening wore on.

I wet the bed again and woke up cold and soaked. As my mother changed the bedding, I started to cry.

"What's wrong Harmony?" she asked softly when she tucked me up in bed and turned off the light. "I'm not angry with you. It was an accident." She gently stroked my forehead, and I felt safe.

"Mama," I whispered, "Mr O'Neal, put his hand up my skirt today."

Somehow I couldn't bring myself to say he'd put his hand inside my knickers and did it every day.

"I don't like it, Mama."

She took me in her arms and held me tight. "Don't worry it won't happen again."

I cuddled into her and felt safe.

"You're a good girl for telling me."

My father had been away working and when he came back late on Saturday after the show, I heard them quietly talking. Their voices were low so I couldn't hear everything being said but heard Mr O'Neal's name whispered.

I was worried, perhaps my father would be angry with me. But the following morning he said nothing about it, in fact, it was never spoken of for years until I was a grown-up, and I brought it up.

My mother was right, it never happened again. Mr O'Neal never put his hand up my skirt or into my knickers again.

But as a result of what happened next, I changed. By the end of school on Monday, I was convinced I had done something wicked and Sister Agatha was right, I was a wicked girl.

The memory still hurts each time I think of what was done to me against my will by an adult I had liked and trusted. For many years, though I believed I was not to blame, I carried a niggling guilt in my heart that there was something wrong with me and it was all my fault.

Telling myself I was not to blame for what Mr O'Neal did to me, and believing it deep in my core, were two different things. What Mr O'Neal did to me can never be totally expunged, and his abuse was further compounded by the abuse I received at school, for telling.

I had been right to be afraid. Apart from my parents who did something about it, the grown-ups at school didn't believe me. I learned children were not believed if grown-ups said something different. I learned grown-ups could lie and they would be believed because they were grown-ups.

Knowing Mr O'Neal had done the same things to the other girls in my class, knowing I wasn't the only one, did nothing to diminish the guilt I felt.

Now decades later, I finally feel able to write this account without pain and the lingering anger I had carried within me for decades.

CHAPTER 14

The day it happened, the day Sister Agatha and I crossed swords for the very last time, started like any other day. But by the end of school, my life would never be the same again. Strangely enough, my anger was not so much with Mr O'Neal, though he was the perpetrator, a cruel wicked man who had groomed, and intimidated us girls and had got away with sexual abuse, but more with Sister Agatha who punished us cruelly for telling the truth. Each time I kneel in prayer and my knees hurt, I am reminded of her.

The day Sister Agatha tried to destroy me began as any normal Monday. It was as expected, a day filled with fear. Assembly took place as usual in the small passage outside the classrooms. It was a long passage leading at one end to the cloakrooms, where we hung our coats, and the other end to the staffroom. All the classrooms doors opened onto the length of the passage and were high ceilinged with tall Victorian windows overlooking the main road.

Sister Agatha had in her sights one of the older girls from the big children's class across the playground. Her name was Josephine but everyone except Sister Agatha called her Josie. Assembly started with Sister Agatha telling Josie off for talking and I looked round to see a sullen look pass over Josie's face.

"And you can take the stupid look off your face, Josephine Devlin," Sister Agatha shouted. "You should be setting a good example for the younger ones, not showing yourself up."

Josie looked down and said nothing.

Sister Agatha stood on a small dais beside the upright piano in the corner. From her position Sister Agatha could see everyone and her eyes missed nothing. Sister Cuthbert sat at the piano her back half turned to us as she played the introductory hymn.

Following prayers and a hymn, Sister Agatha started her usual list of complaints and threats. It was Monday morning, and the usual question was trotted out.

"Hands up all of you who didn't go to Mass on Sunday?"

A few hands shot up. Mine stayed well down though I hadn't been to Mass for weeks. My mother was ill and had been told to rest but I was never going to be so stupid as to admit it.

Sister Agatha, her hands waving in front of her was working herself up into a rage. "It is a mortal sin not to go to Mass on Sunday. A mortal sin is an indelible mark on your soul." Her eyes swept over us. "It means you can never get rid of the black mark and when you die, you will have to go to Hell, forever."

I shuddered. Hell! Not even Purgatory. What hope did I have? Although Purgatory was a bad as Hell, it was temporary. But then again, there was no clear timeline of how long you would have to stay in Purgatory. Souls particularly murky souls with a lot of sins would have to stay until the end of the world. And those black souls, really black with mortal sins, would have to go to Hell forever. Black was not a good colour for your Soul to be. Black Souls were doomed to everlasting torture. Black was bad.

"Don't forget, God will judge if you are good enough to go to Heaven. If your Soul is filled with too many black marks, you won't go to Heaven." Sister Agatha sounded almost gleeful. God sounded really cruel. I thought he was supposed to love us.

I stopped thinking about sins and watched her face as she spoke and wondered if she wanted Heaven all to herself.

I quaked at the thought of the lies I had told. Not only hadn't I been to Mass for several weeks, but also I had lied every Monday morning for weeks. Would God be very angry with me?

"All those with their hands up will come and see me at playtime." Her face red and her cane hand, momentarily devoid of a cane, twitched restlessly.

Seeing Sister Agatha at playtime meant getting the cane.

I looked around at the expressions of terror on the faces of the guilty and was curious as to why they admitted to not going to Mass? As far as I was concerned, telling the truth to Sister Agatha was dangerous, and lying was well worth extra time in Purgatory.

To catch us out, Sister Agatha would sometimes point to someone with his or her hand down and ask them what the sermon had been about. If they couldn't answer, they would be accused of lying and made to join the ranks of the non-Mass goers, for punishment later.

Tell me what child ever listens to a sermon? Most grown-ups don't listen to sermons either; it was usually a good time to daydream about something else. But in our Monday morning world, keeping our hand down was as much a risk as raising it. A risk I thought well worth taking.

Admitting to Sister Agatha, I hadn't been to Mass on Sunday was nothing short of stupidity, and even though I couldn't read, I wasn't stupid.

CHAPTER 15

Sister Agatha appeared to enjoy having us all stand before her quaking in our shoes. She hadn't finished castigating those recalcitrant sinners whose hands were still waving like flags in the air, for missing Mass.

Her voice strident, she continued. "I recognise the same children each week putting up their hands. You come to a Catholic school," she railed. "You must go to Mass on Sunday, otherwise, you won't be welcome here. You must make sure to tell your parents to take you next Sunday or you will be in more trouble. Do you understand?"

Small heads nodded eagerly and a chorus of frightened voices rang out. "Yes, Sister." The unfortunates who would receive the cane during playtime hung their heads, their expression mingled with shame and misery as they fixed their eyes on the floor.

"And don't forget to tell the priest when you next go to confession, you..." Sister Agatha's tirade halted abruptly, her eyes squinted at us. We all stiffened. What now?

She moved her head, bent forward and sniffed. Her head slowly moved from side to side as a predator alerted to a prey in its vicinity. She then lifted her head and sniffed the air again her features twisted, her nose twitched. She had been distracted by a smell. Her eyes swept accusingly over us.

"Someone here has brought dog's mess into school."

No one moved. A profound hush fell over us. The air stilled as fear shrouded us.

Sister Agatha's long nose twisted upwards as she shouted, "I can smell it." Her eyes blazed with fury. She looked towards the group of teachers clustered to her left. "You can smell it too," she stated.

They looked startled, shuffled closer together and nodded eagerly. It was then, I realized, they too were frightened of her.

"Who is the bold person bringing dog mess into our school?"

Her eyes swept over us ready to pinpoint some poor individual and cast blame. Heads quickly hung as everyone tried to avoid her eyes. The smell of fear in the air was almost tangible, far greater than any smell of dog poo.

No one moved, not even to let out the breath they were holding. Who was going to admit to such a heinous crime as stepping in dog poo and then walking it into school?

No one.

"I want you all to look at the bottom of your shoes and the person responsible will put up their hand."

There was a wild shuffling as children lifted their feet, looked at the soles of their shoes all the while praying they were not the culprit. Our teachers in the corner didn't move.

Someone at the back, one of the big girls whispered something to the girl next to her and they both giggled.

Sister Agatha's head shot up, like a hungry hyena homing in on its prey. She fastened cold eyes on the tall dark-haired girl at the back of the passage.

"Josephine Devlin if you have something to say, we would all like to hear it."

Dread hung in the air soaking up hope. Something bad was about to happen and in expectation, all heads turned to look at Josie. The entire school waited.

Josie was in the top class. She would be leaving school when the term ended in the summer. She was one of the big girls. She was nearly fifteen. Always in trouble, Josie didn't care what she said to teachers, I'd even seen her pull faces at them behind their backs. Sister Agatha told her constantly she would come to no good. And if she didn't pull her socks up, she would not give her a good reference for a job. I wasn't sure what a reference was, but Josie used to shrug as though she didn't care.

"Well, we are all waiting." Her voice chilly with menace Sister Agatha lifted her head even higher and fastened her eyes on Josie. "No one is leaving this assembly until you share your comments with us."

Josie gave an exaggerated sigh, flicked back her dark hair and threw a look of utter boredom at the faces turned towards her. Then she calmly lifted her head and looked straight into Sister Agatha's face.

"I said it was lucky to step in dog poo." Her voice rang out over the heads of the whole school. We gasped.

"Lucky? Lucky is it, you bold girl?" Sister Agatha screeched. A titter rose from the top class. "We'll see how lucky it is. You will spend your playtime going around the school cleaning up any mess you see and picking up any rubbish. And then you'll come and see me."

I liked Josie immediately although I never spoke to her. To this day I applaud her for her bravery in the line of fire. I wanted to be like Josie when I got older.

After the assembly incident, I would watch Josie on the play-ground. She was loud and would shriek with laughter if she thought something was funny. Josie didn't mind where she made a noise and Sister Agatha often came out of her office to tell her, she sounded like a fishwife.

Josie would shrug and look at Sister Agatha with an expression of patent dislike. I can't begin to say how much I admired her.

But the day of the dog poo got a lot worse quite unexpectedly, and in a way, I would never have anticipated, even in my wildest dreams.

CHAPTER 16

W e returned to class after all the excitement of Josie and the dog poo, and as I sat gazing out of the window I wished I were somewhere else...anywhere else. I dreaded the thought of Mr O'Neal calling me up to his desk to mark my book. I wished he would leave me alone. I wished he would stop putting his hand up my skirt and into my knickers. I chewed my lips with anxiety and my stomach clenched with fear.

It was a perfect spring day, the sun was shining and I longed to be outside, away from school, away from Mr O'Neal and away from Sister Agatha.

I cast a quick look to the front of the class where Mr O'Neal sat and gave a sigh of relief. I was safe for the moment as Mr O'Neal was busy marking a boy's book. I turned back to stare out of the window and cupped my chin in my hands then suppressed an inaudible gasp of surprise.

I saw Uncle Clive turn into the school gates and walk around the corner and out of view towards Sister Agatha's office. Uncle Clive was my father's brother.

What was he doing coming to my school? He had never been to my school before. I kept a watch on the gates expecting to see him leave, but then we were all told to get ready for our Times-Table test and I missed seeing him leave. Seeing him turn up at school set my nerves jangling. Was something wrong at home?

It was later, years later, when I asked my father why Uncle Clive had been the one to come to school, he told me, he'd been booked to play at the Winter Gardens Theatre in Bournemouth for the week and was unable to go to the school himself. My mother couldn't go because her blood pressure had shot up over the weekend and she'd been taken to hospital after we had gone to school. He'd asked Uncle Clive go and tell Sister Agatha about Mr O'Neal putting his hand up my skirt.

It was just after Mr O'Neal started the Times-Tables test that Sister Agatha threw open the door and without a word to Mr O'Neal marched to the front of the class her shoes squeaking loudly. She glared around at us and her eyes finally settled on me.

"Harmony Brown," she said.

Alarmed, I quaked with fear. Something terrible had happened. Had Uncle Clive come to collect me? Had Mama died?

"Will you excuse me, Mr O'Neal," Sister Agatha said as she turned belatedly to look at him. "I want to have a word with the girls. All the girls."

"Yes Sister," Mr O'Neal replied his face creasing with anxiety. His cheeks had reddened as though caught out doing something naughty and he hovered unsure what he was meant to do next.

"You can take the boys outside for French cricket," Sister Agatha instructed authoritatively. He immediately jumped to attention. She stepped towards him and whispered something in his ear.

Mr O'Neal ordered the boys to line up by the door whilst us girls remained standing behind our desks.

I looked at the boys longingly. It was such a lovely sunny spring morning and being able to go outside and play French cricket would have been a great treat. I envied the boys.

As Mr O'Neal left the room with the boys and shut the door behind them, he looked over his shoulder and his eyes met mine. His look was one of threat and I wasn't sure what it meant.

I immediately thought he knew I was going to be told some terrible news because my mother wasn't well. But why such news should be imparted with only the girls present, I couldn't understand? I bit hard on my lower lip and held my breath.

Sister Agatha removed Mr O'Neal's chair from behind his desk and placed it in front of us. She sat heavily, her back as straight as a ramrod, her arms tucked into the large sleeves of her black habit, the toes of her shiny black shoes peeped out from the hem of her skirt.

Several minutes passed as she looked around at us all. "Now." She pulled her shoulders back and smoothed her long black skirt over her knees. "I want all you girls to move forward. Come on, move to the front." She pointed to desks in the front row. "I want you all in separate desks."

There was a chaotic banging of chairs as girls shuffled forward and slipped onto seats behind desks in the front row.

"That's right, girls." She turned, and her small beady eyes fell on me. "No, not you Harmony Brown, I want you here." She pointed with her index finger to a spot a few inches from her knees.

I shook with fear as I moved forward to stand before her.

"Not there, you bold wicked child. I don't want to look at your face."

Her face contorted with dislike as she pointed to her side. "Kneel down there in front of the Virgin Mary."

She pointed to a small statue on a low table at the left-hand corner of the class. "Kneel there and pray the Virgin Mary will forgive you for your evil, wicked, pagan ways."

Wordlessly I knelt on the hardwood floor my back to the rest of the girls and Sister Agatha to my right.

"Now girls..." Sister Agatha bent forward as though she was about to impart a secret of momentous importance. "How many of you girls have been talking to Harmony Brown?"

Each time she said my name the words were spat out with such venom it was as though she was trying to empty her mouth of a particularly noxious taste.

No one moved and silence mingled with fear cloaked us all. Of course, they'd been talking to me, but who was going to admit it. Talking to me about what? She made it sound as though talking to me was about to be listed as one of the great mortal sins in line with missing Mass on Sunday.

"Come on now. I know Harmony Brown has been going around spreading wicked lies about one of our best teachers. So which of you girls has she been talking to?"

Silence greeted her words.

"You don't have to be afraid to tell the truth. Harmony Brown can't do anything to you if you tell the truth. I know she is an immodest dirty girl who has been telling lies and I want to know who she has been talking to about those lies."

Her words were again met with silence.

"I am prepared to sit here all day until you confess to what Harmony Brown has been saying." Her hands slid up each sleeve of her habit covering their pale bluish white flesh.

No one moved. No one spoke.

"May the good Lord forgive you Harmony Brown for your evil ways in corrupting these girls," she hissed as she turned to me. "Don't look at me. Don't you dare take your eyes off the Virgin Mary, you bold immodest girl."

All the girls sat in silence. I trembled and struggled to stay upright on my knees. Kneeling on the hardwood floorboards had begun to hurt and it felt as though my knees were burning. I longed to stand, longed to relieve the pressure of the hardwood beneath them, by rubbing them. It felt as though my knees were on fire.

It was true. Mr O'Neal had done those things to me. I hadn't lied. Had my telling my mother about Mr O'Neal made me immodest? Maybe just talking about it was immodest. If I had said nothing, would I be wicked and immodest?

All I could think of as I knelt, aware of the blood thrumming in my ears, waiting for someone to speak, was I wouldn't be suffering now if I had said nothing about Mr O'Neal. This was my fault. Everything was my fault.

Mr O' Neal would say I liked it. Perhaps he would say I made him do it. And I would get into trouble because grown-ups were never wrong. Sister Agatha would believe him, not me.

Perhaps it would have been all right as long as I hadn't talked about it, hadn't told anyone. But I hadn't liked it. I had wanted him to stop.

CHAPTER 17

I knelt, my knees burning with pain, and listened as Sister Agatha moved the wooden rosary beads through her fingers. I lowered my eyes and looked sideways watching her lips move in silent prayer and wondered what she was saying to the Virgin Mary.

My eyes returned to focus on the statue of the Virgin Mary before me, pink-faced and beautiful. Whose prayers would the Virgin Mary listen to, Sister Agatha's or mine? Somehow I didn't feel too confident.

"Don't look at me," Sister Agatha hissed as she caught the slight movement of my head. And as though she had the ability to read my thoughts, added, "I'm praying for your Soul."

Silence fell again, and I turned my attention back to the statue of the Virgin Mary and examined its every detail. The blond-haired, blue-eyed, pink-cheeked Virgin Mary was dressed in a white satin gown with a blue cloak flowing from her shoulders down to her feet. Every class had a statue of the Virgin Mary.

Would she still love me if I were immodest? I wanted her to love me, to take me to heaven when I died. But it looked as though telling Mama about Mr O'Neal putting his hand up my skirt made me immodest, and the Virgin Mary wouldn't love me or take me to

Heaven. I told myself I shouldn't care. If getting into Heaven meant I had to have Mr O'Neal's hands touching me inside my knickers than I wouldn't like Heaven anyway.

Somehow the statue of the Virgin Mary reminded me of Mary Murphy, at least in the colour of her hair and pink cheeks.

Mary Murphy was the least favourite girl in my book, for no other reason than she was one of Sister Agatha's favourite.

Mary could do no wrong. She was always chosen to play the Virgin Mary in the Christmas nativity play along with Patrick O'Shea who was always Joseph. Patrick was also blue-eyed and blond-haired an ideal counterpart to Mary Murphy in her role as the Virgin Mary.

If Sister Agatha's version of the nativity was anything to go by, Joseph never knew Mary was going to have a baby until after he'd married her. It was then the Angel Gabriel told him.

I had no idea at the time, that the Virgin May's name was actually just Mary, and the *Virgin* part was a description of her condition. I thought *Virgin* was a special holy name.

Well it didn't matter what I thought. Sister Agatha was off again just as I was beginning to enjoy the silence, enjoy being wrapped up in my own thoughts a world away from the pain in my knees. Sister Agatha was relentless in her determination to sniff out the evil permeating her school, in other words, evidence, I, Harmony Brown, was hand in glove with the devil.

"We will now all say the Rosary and ask the Virgin Mary to look into our souls and gives us the strength, to tell the truth." She sniffed loudly. "All kneel," she ordered imperiously.

Each girl slid from her seat onto her knees. Sister Agatha remained seated as all the girls knelt before her. "We will say the Sorrowful Mysteries to remind us Jesus gave his life on the cross for our sins."

She pulled her rosary onto her lap. "The first sorrowful mystery, the Agony of Jesus in the Garden." She made the sign of the cross. "Our Father who ..."

We joined together to say the *Lord's Prayer*, followed by ten *Hail Mary's*, and one *Glory be to God*. She went through all five decades; the Agony in the Garden, Jesus is scourged at the Pillar, Jesus Crowned with Thorns, Jesus Carries the Cross and finally the Crucifixion of Jesus. Each decade entailed, one *Our Father*, ten *Hail Mary's* and One *Glory be to God*.

The chanting of prayers was a welcome relief, as no words of condemnation or threats came out of Sister Agatha's mouth whilst she was praying. As the last *Glory be to the Father* was intoned, Sister Agatha sat back.

"Sit," she commanded. The girls silently clambered back onto their seats. "Now are you all ready to tell the truth?"

No one spoke, and she gave a deep sigh of frustration.

"Who has Harmony Brown been telling lies to, about our Mr O'Neal?"

I longed to turn and see who was going to tell lies about me as I strongly expected someone would, simply to get into Sister Agatha's good books. Fear of punishment, fear of the cane would strain the truth. It would take a very brave person indeed, to tell the truth. I accepted I was alone.

"Mary my child," Sister Agatha said gently. "Your hand is up. Say what you have to say, child. The Virgin Mary will be happy you are the only truthful girl here."

My heart sank. I might have guessed, Sister Agatha's favourite, Mary Murphy was about to tell a bunch of lies about me.

"I knew, I could rely on you to have the strength, to tell the truth." Sister Agatha continued encouragingly.

Mary gave a little cough, "Mr O'Neil put his hand up my skirt too," she announced loudly. Her voice quivered as the words came out of her mouth, but she stood with her head held high.

I looked over my shoulder shocked. Someone had told the truth! The expression on Sister Agatha's face was one of disbelief vying with rage. Her wimple quivered, her face turned bright red and her hands clutched at the rosary on her lap.

CHAPTER 18

I watched with fear as Sister Agatha's mouth opened and no words emerged. She went a horrible colour of even deeper red and looked as though she may be chocking. Finally, she appeared to gather strength from somewhere and words, angry words emerged from her thin lips.

"Lord have mercy on *you*, child. You have been corrupted by evil. You had better kneel down next to your friend and pray the Virgin Mary will save your soul."

The word, *friend*, was said with an edge to it, implying I was evil and Mary Murphy would be kneeling next to the devil personified.

"I want you both to say the act of contrition. You must ask the Virgin Mary to ask her son, Jesus Christ to forgive you for your wicked lies."

Mary stepped from behind her desk and knelt silently beside me, clasped her hands together in prayer and fixed her gaze steadily on the statue of the Virgin Mary. I slid her a sideways glance, shocked she had told the truth. She was staring at the statue of the Virgin Mary as her lips moved in prayer.

Sister Agatha's eyes settled firmly on me. "Evil has come into this class and corrupted our innocence." She sniffed. "I want you two girls, to think about little Saint Maria Goretti. She was hardly any older than you, yet she chose death rather than be immodest...rather than be corrupted.

I knew the story of Saint Maria Goretti, who didn't? Sister Agatha had told us on numerous occasions how a child had spurned an evil man rather than risk Hell. Sister Agatha in her telling of the story of Saint Maria Goretti had emphasised how the twelve-year-old peasant girl had so impressed the Pope, he'd by-passed the beatification stage. And without waiting for the obligatory three miracles had granted Maria Goretti sainthood status.

Later, I read that, poor little Maria Goretti was stabbed and murdered by the son of a farmhand. She had rejected and fought against his sexual attack and was killed. She'd had no choice in the manner of her death.

Maria Goretti had done nothing wrong. She was a victim. I was a victim too, very much a victim as Saint Maria Goretti had been.

But at the time Sister Agatha was rebuking me for being wicked and immodest, I had no idea being immodest, could be foisted on children by an adult, and was certainly not a choice.

I shook with fear at the mention of Maria Goretti's choice to die. Was I expected to die? Would she believe me if I died? I looked at Sister Agatha, at her large pasty face surrounded by crinkly white starched material overhung at the back by a black veil, her lips drawn back in a snarl, her large sharp teeth exposed, and I knew what the devil looked like, and it wasn't me.

Sister Agatha spoke again turning to the pale frightened faces of the group seated in the front row. "We will punish those that spread immodest lies."

The clink and clunk of Sister Agatha's rosary beads could be heard again from beneath the black shroud she wore. It was then the dinner bell rang and we were instructed to rise and line up by the door.

"You Harmony Brown," Sister Agatha shouted as I made an attempt at escape. "Get to the back of the line."

She strode to the head of the line, and swung back to face us, her small round wire-rimmed glasses glinted in the sun glancing off the tall windows of the classroom as she peered at us. I didn't miss the look of hate in her eyes or the expression of unconcealed fury her face betrayed.

"If anyone of you tries to talk to Harmony, you will be severely punished. And if I see any of you talking to anyone...anyone, do you hear, you will be punished, *do* you understand me?"

With those words, she led us smartly across the playground to the dining-hall in silence. We were served cold watery lumpy mashed potato, limp cold pale cabbage, along with something greasy and runny, called, mince meat.

The dinner ladies carelessly slopped the food on our plates as we moved in a silent line along the trestle table and then carried our plate to a long trestle table set aside for us. Sister Agatha stood overseeing our meal. When we had finished our lunch, we were led back to the classroom again in silence.

We had no playtime break. In fact, we'd had no morning break or afternoon break either. We had been sent out, one at a time to the toilet and had returned to the classroom for more chastisement. Sister Agatha wanted to break our spirit, but all she got was silence.

Mary and I were told to take up our allotted places in front of the Statue of the Virgin Mary once more. The other girls were told to sit and think about how wicked they were not to denounce the lies told about such a good man, their teacher. I could hear the happy laughing voices of the children at play outside and wished with all my heart I was outside playing. This was torture.

Mary was asked several times to retract what she had said and confess she had told a lie under the influence of Harmony Brown. She remained silent.

We all stayed silent until the end of the day with silence only broken from time to time by Sister Agatha promising me eternal flames for my lies and wicked corrupting ways.

Whilst we'd been kept in isolation, the boys played numerous games of French cricket with Mr O'Neal. And when the bell announcing the end of the day rang, the girls were sent back to their desks. The boys flushed and happy came in to collect their belongings before lining up to leave. There was no sign of Mr O'Neal. Sister Agatha looked over the group of girls before her and shook her head disapprovingly.

"Stand for prayers," she commanded and turned to the tableau of us forced penitents in front of the statue of the Virgin Mary. "Mary and Harmony, you too."

We scrambled to our feet keeping our heads down.

"We will start with the Prayer of Contrition and then you can all go home. But I'm warning you girls," she moved forward her finger wagging at all of us. "You are not allowed to talk about this to anyone...anyone. Do you understand? If you ever talk about this again, I will know and you will be severely punished."

She waited as heads nodded. "If I hear any more about this matter, I will know where it comes from."

A group of girls from the other classes lingered by the gate in the bottom playground and as our class emerged they ran towards us, curiosity etched on their faces.

"What happened?" they chorused. They'd heard Sister Agatha had been with us all day, and we had not even been allowed playtime.

"Nothing," we all chorused back and I turned and walked down the hill towards home. I couldn't wait to get as far away as possible from all the girls in my class. They had sat silent, and had been prepared to watch as I had been punished. I scanned the school gate and play-ground for Mary but she was nowhere to be seen.

"We are not allowed to talk about it." I heard a girl say as I quick-ened my step. I didn't want to compound my sins by being immodest again by talking about what Mr O'Neal had done to me and so hurried out of the gate.

After that day, I had a new respect for Mary Murphy, though we never spoke. In fact to this day, I can't remember either of us saying anything to one another.

After supper Aunt Olga, who'd come to look after me whilst Mama was in the hospital, tucked me up in bed and I felt a deep sense of relief at being home. She sang a Nat King Cole song about love as I drifted off to sleep content I was safe once more. I didn't wet the bed that night.

CHAPTER 19

I remember that day in March when I knelt in front of the statue of the blond pink-cheeked Virgin Mary for the entire day, as though it was yesterday. But I don't remember Sister Agatha ever speaking to me again, at least, not directly.

Mr O'Neal never spoke to me again either and from what I can remember, never marked any of my books. I never had to worry about him putting his hand up my skirt because he never came near me. I was told, some years later, he had moved to teach in a boy's boarding school, a Seminary. I'm not sure whether it was true or not, but whatever happened, I hope no one else ever suffered the way I had. I speculate he never changed and to this day, I feel great pity for the boys he taught.

The following year I failed my Eleven Plus disastrously.

I remember sitting at my desk in a silent classroom and being warned we were not allowed to cheat. We were handed some papers and told to write our name at the top of the page, read what was printed on the papers carefully and answer the questions.

"You are to keep your eyes on your work and not copy anyone's," Sister Agatha instructed sweeping us all with a stern look.

I wrote my name and then my eyes fell on what looked like hieroglyphics before me. I recognised two words, *and,* and *the.*

As I bent forward to make an attempt to write, I heard Sister Agatha screaming at Francis Doyle. "You have been copying some-one's work." She snatched the paper from Francis' desk and waved it in front of her. "Haven't you?"

Francis shook her head, tears welling up in her eyes. I looked across at her and saw her face redden with humiliation.

"Don't lie. Don't you dare lie to me. You didn't even have the sense to write your own name, you stupid girl."

She threw the paper back at Francis, turned and walked away.

Francis put her face down on her arms and sobbed.

She was ignored.

In the playground afterwards, I heard Patrick O'Shea telling everyone how easy it was and I moved away before he saw me. He whispered something as Francis came into view and everyone around him laughed.

I wasn't surprised at my terrible results. My mother, when she received the notification of my failure, asked, "Did you do your best Harmony?"

"Yes Mama," I replied.

She took me in her arms and kissed me. "That's all I ask."

I'm sure when I finally left the school, Sister Agatha was relieved to see me go.

It had become increasingly difficult to hide the hate in my eyes each time I looked at her. I knew hate was a bad thing, but I did hate her with every fibre of my being. I was in no doubt Sister Agatha hated me too.

To this day I have never understood how someone dedicated to living a life of love, acceptance and forgiveness in the name of Jesus Christ, could show such cruelty and hate towards an innocent child. Perhaps my refusal to be cowered by her infuriated her, or maybe it was because being *coloured* was in some way an indication of evil.

As the summer holiday approached and I knew I wasn't ever going back and would never see Sister Agatha or Mr O'Neal again, I felt almost dizzy with happiness.

CHAPTER 20

Time moved on. I changed school and was happy. When I was fifteen, my mother sent me to the Convent boarding school in the South of England she had attended as a child. But not before I fell in love.

He was the first and only true love in my life. I was fifteen and adored the feeling of loving and being loved. And best of all he was West Indian and understood me intuitively. He knew where I was coming from and understood what it was like to be black and a minority. He was the first black boy I had met and I loved it. He gave me my first kiss, something I never forgot. But I still felt guilty about Mr O'Neal... I still felt what he did to me was somehow my fault. I couldn't shake off the feeling of guilt and somehow being unclean and being bad. Mr O'Neal came between me, and the boy I loved.

To further complicate the issue, my parents weren't happy about my relationship. My mother was greatly concerned he wasn't Catholic, and she foretold of catastrophic problems if I ended up with him. He and I wrote to each other daily and my father would rush to the post and demand my letter, which he would read. He would then question me in detail about every aspect of the letter. "Has he kissed you? Did he French kiss you? Did he touch you?"

What was French kissing? I didn't know. And neither did I know touching me should somehow be wrong. Of course, he touched me. He put his arm round me when he kissed me, didn't he? I felt I was somehow immoral. His questions were intrusive and suspicious, and he made me feel my strong emotions were wrong and grubby. In the end, I couldn't even speak to the one I loved so much.

I met him many years later and by then he was already married. I knew it was too late for us. He had met and loved someone else. I would never hurt another woman even though my feelings had not changed. We never met again.

I went to the same boarding school my mother's father had sent her to when she was seven. The nuns had kept her until she was eighteen, five years after her father had died and her fees were no longer paid. They had treated her with affection and many of the older nuns still remembered their little '*Topsy*,' as they'd called her.

The nuns were different from Sister Agatha, a different order too. They were kind, and I never saw any sort of physical punishment metered out, no matter what anyone did.

I never found any need to be a *bold girl*, except when I would sneak out every now and again to buy fish and chips, an activity strictly forbidden. There were times the food served up for supper was beyond redemption and growing girls need food they enjoyed eating.

Twice during my time there, I come up against authority and both times, food was involved. On one occasion I had refused to eat my apple crumble at lunch as it had inadvertently been served with the same spoon used to serve the mince stew. I objected to mince mixed with stewed apple and was prepared to sit it out, rather than have a mouthful of mince tainted apple crumble pass my lips.

Reverend Mother eventually arrived in the dining room, now empty of on-lookers. Lessons had started, and I was still sitting over my apple crumble tasting of a strange mixture of mince and sweet apple.

"My dear," she said softly as she slid onto the bench opposite me. "Sister Lucy Joseph tells me you are refusing to finish your lunch."

I nodded. "Yes Reverend Mother," I returned calmly. I liked

Reverend Mother, who didn't? She always treated everyone with a gentle respect, no matter who they were or what they'd done.

"Look at it," I said pointing indignantly at my plate. "It's disgusting. No one should have to eat apple crumble mixed with mince."

"My dear, it's food," she returned gently.

Reverend Mother always started or ended her sentences with *my dear* and liberally interspersed *my dears* throughout. In all the time I was under Reverend Mother's care I never heard her do otherwise.

On this occasion she sat silent, observing me until I dropped my eyes to my plate of now cold, congealed apple crumble and custard with specks of mince.

"My dear," she repeated softly. "Food is necessary to sustain our body. We are lucky to have food on our plate. We must not forget to thank God."

She gave a plaintive sigh, neither agreeing nor disagreeing with my assessment of the disgusting mass on my plate.

"There are many who will go without food today. Many of our brothers and sisters in Africa have not eaten for many days. Many babies will die of hunger before the day is out." She paused and looked at me.

I regarded my dish with disgust and shame swamped me at my ingratitude. How was I going to get out of this, without looking as though I was giving in?

We both sat in silence for a while longer. Me, uncomfortable as I regarded my selfish attitude towards the riches on my plate in the form of apple crumble and mince, and Reverend Mother, her soft eyes watching me, with no hint of anger or criticism.

"My dear," she continued after a pause. "Let us say a prayer of thanks for the food we are given and promise not to waste what others need."

I squirmed uncomfortably and played with my spoon begging silently for the humiliating ordeal to end.

"Thank you, Lord, for the food we eat..." Reverend Mother intoned. I was lost in shame and didn't hear much about the food I was to be grateful for, yet aware somewhere in her prayer were the words hunger, dying and forgive me. I joined her in the, *Amen.*

"Now my dear," she said. "I think you should eat a spoonful of your food, just to show God you don't mean to be wasteful."

"Yes Reverend Mother," I mumbled capitulating. I felt so utterly ungrateful and guilty. I had reached a point where I would have eaten the entire plateful and cleaned off any remaining morsel of food. Reverend Mother had gently given me a way out, without my losing face. The spoonful of food I placed in my mouth seemed minuscule and I was elated to leave the dining room and return to my lessons.

"Thank you, my dear," she said as I rose to leave.

I felt chastened and humbled throughout the rest of the day and still have great respect for the woman who allowed everyone to win. There were no losers in Reverend Mother's view. In her book, everyone had to win. She was a Win-Win negotiator long before the term was born. She had won, and to some extent so had I.

CHAPTER 21

Reverend Mother hadn't finished with me. I saw her a few more times during my journey through school.

She once caught me returning from the fish and chip shop in the town. She didn't lecture me for breaking the rules by leaving the Convent grounds without permission. Instead, she led me into the refectory collected a plate on the way and indicated I should place the fish and chips on the plate. She then retrieved a knife and fork, handed them to me and sat opposite.

"My dear, why?" She asked softly.

Finding it difficult to admit I'd only taken a tiny portion of the supper because it was unusually unappetizing, I hung my head and stared down at the huge mound of chips on my plate. Somehow, I had lost my appetite.

"I was just being greedy Reverend Mother," I confessed. What else could I say? Could I admit I hated the food we'd been served and enjoyed the adventure of sneaking out to the fish and chip shop for lovely greasy chips? No, of course not.

"My dear," she said gently, eyes peering bird-like at me over her half-framed spectacles. "Remember, it is good to always leave the table feeling a little hungry."

Those were the wisest words I have ever heard said...words said by a little old woman, thin and frail, whom I was told ate like a sparrow and lived well into her nineties.

I think of her to this day, and each time I step on the scales to weigh myself, I vow to leave the table feeling a *little hungry*.

Reams and reams have been written about diets and how to lose weight, yet Reverend Mother had the most logical diet ever designed. Her words were the most profound I have ever heard on the subject of healthy living.

Profound though she might have been on the subject of food, somehow her lessons on sex lacked conviction.

I'd had in my possession a book by Françoise Sagan, *A Certain Smile*, and I'd enjoyed it so much I passed it on to my friends. Somehow it had reached Reverend Mother's hands. I've never quite worked out how? But in every group of girls there is always a snitch.

When she gathered us all together in the library it was evident she had read it. We knew Reverend Mother was going to give us a talk, and having no idea what was so important as to cancel lessons, we irreverently agreed between us to count how many, *my dears*, she uttered and we put in our bets.

"My dears," she began.

One, we counted.

"I've been given one of your books, my dears."

Two, we counted.

Poor Reverend Mother, she had probably been ushered out of chapel because Sister Elizabeth had caught one of us with a book, not on the approved list. Reverend Mother was eighty, ancient to us seventeen-year-olds.

"My dears," she continued.

Three.

She held up the book. I squirmed with embarrassment. Did she know it was my book? Would I get into trouble?

"It is important to know..." she began as she stood before us, "...there are some books that are not wise for you to read."

I looked down at my shoes. Since I had learned to read, I read everything and anything I laid my hands on. What did she mean? Did there exist some books we shouldn't read?

It was no use playing the innocent, I knew which books were frowned upon, at least some of them. I actively sorted out books that were banned by the Catholic Church.

On this occasion, Reverend Mother gave a little cough as she laid the book on the desk next to her. "You may start reading a book, but..." she stopped and looked at us. "If you come to a point in the story where people start to take off their clothes, it's time to close the book, and find another more suitable book." She paused as though trying to gather her thoughts then her eyes slid vaguely over us.

A surprised gasp pulsated through the group. We knew her hearing wasn't too good, and she appeared not to have heard the faint flutter of air escaping our lungs. I for one knew, without a doubt, should I reach a page where men and women were taking off their clothes, it would be the point at which, I would have extreme difficulty putting the book down.

"Now my dears." She drew in a deep breath as though she'd walked up a long hill and had stopped to gather strength for the next push to the top. "It's time we talked about ... er...." She paused again.

We were silent fearing the slightest movement, the slightest sound would distract her from her thoughts and she wouldn't get to the good bits...we suspected would be about sex!

"My dears, you will soon be going out into the world. I think it's time we talked about..." her eyes swept over us again, "er...Men."

Our hearts leapt with expectation. We watched Reverend Mother our eyes bright as ripples of excitement vibrated through us. Was she going to talk about sex? A sex lesson, from a woman who had very likely entered the Convent aged fifteen, innocent, with no knowledge of men, love or sex, would be incredible. We could hardly wait. Our eager faces, eyes bright with expectation, focused on her in palpable anticipation. Curiosity about such an exciting and forbidden activity as sex consumed us.

We were pubescent girls with raging hormones, hungering for contact with the opposite sex. Men were alien, dangerous and therefore exciting. In our minds, *men equated to sex*. The two were synonymous and so thrilling. We knew nothing about sex, but it sounded electrifyingly dangerous.

What did Reverend Mother know about sex? As a Bride of Christ and from the way she approached it, men and sex were something alien. The very word, *sex*, must have been an anathema to her. Yet she had a duty to perform, being officially responsible for the girls before her, and she took her responsibility seriously. She would do her duty, whatever the cost to herself.

We were sheltered girls, innocent in all but thought. We were eager to find out the secrets of the species called, *men*, and even more, we were hoping to be introduced to the activity called sex. We waited with baited breath.

"My dears," she said. We had long stopped counting her *my dears*, and in a half-hour talk, she fumbled vaguely through the meaning of life, sex and men. Her most memorable decree on men has remained with me.

"When you go to dances and meet men, always ask if they are Catholics, my dears." She paused, head wobbling from side to side, as though emphasizing a crucial point. "Some men aren't." She stopped, drew in a soft breath, her eyes swept sadly over us as though sharing something so outrageous she wanted us to absorb her words before she continued.

"My dears." Her half spectacles sparkled in the dappled light glinting off the glass in the library windows. Her voice lowered as though she was about to impart the answer to life and the universe, and it was a secret.

"Some men you will meet won't be Catholics."

Was she trying to tell us there were men lurking around who posed a real threat to us uninitiated, innocent girls, and these men were not Catholics?

A bold girl at the back sniggered and Sister Elizabeth eyes raked over us registering the offender for a reprimand later. We waited, knowing there would be more.

"If they're not Catholics, my dears, do not accept the dance." She stopped, gripped her walking stick and wobbled as though she was about to collapse, drained by her pronouncement. Sister Elizabeth darted forward hands outstretched lest Reverend Mother toppled over. But she righted herself, took another deep breath as her fading sight rested on us and took stock.

We sat primly, legs tightly together at the knees, our hands folded neatly on our laps, as would be expected from properly brought up girls. We were decorous young women, eyes wide with unsurpassed excitement.

Reverend Mother looked perpetually confused, probably wondering what the fuss was all about. Wondering where she was? Who were we? Why did she in her dotage, have to talk about sex and men? What was sex anyway?

Another important consideration, when the time came for us to find a good Catholic husband, Reverend Mother stressed, was the age of the likely candidate,.

"My dears," she said, "you need to be careful if you meet a man who is thirty and not yet married. You need to ask him why?"

Thirty! Heaven forbid! Ancient.

Our thoughts fizzed with excitement. Thirty may be ancient, but our curiosity skyrocketed. Notwithstanding their obvious experience by dint of their age, what salacious, wicked secrets did men of thirty have we should not know about?

"If they reach such an age, and are not yet married then you need to be careful."

Oh, how true...how true. It was to take many years for me to appreciate such wisdom. However, I met a few along the way, before I married and asked them why they were still single.

"I haven't met the right girl yet," was the usual reply, with the implication, should I play my cards right, I could be the one.

What did Reverend Mother know about thirty-something men, we did not? It has remained an enigma, intriguing me for years. She believed she didn't have to be in the world, to know the world. She believed her observations from the sideline of life or perhaps heavenly revelations were enough to know what was important about men and sex.

We, on the other hand, weren't convinced.

CHAPTER 22

I liked the opposite sex, longed for them to be interested in me. But I feared deep down, I was really bad and Mr O'Neal had put is hand up my skirt and into my knickers because I was bad. I believed I didn't have a right to be sexually appealing and no one would want me. I kept a secret diary and faithfully documented all my longing and desires. To make matters worse, I was *coloured* and didn't know any *coloured* boys. My first love was gone forever.

Other girls talked about boyfriends they'd met during the school holidays. I didn't have a boyfriend, though I longed for one. I wished I had a boyfriend, someone I could share all my deepest and most private thoughts.

I felt isolated from the girls around me, not always, just sometimes. I would watch them and think how lucky they were not to have had a Mr O'Neal and Sister Agatha in their lives. The memory of what had happened to me when I was ten clung to me like a bad smell and made me different from the other girls. Feeling so disparate from the girls around me, cemented the belief I wouldn't be attractive to the opposite sex.

Perhaps, I decided, if I looked more like them, things would be different. I focused on my hair, if I changed my frizzy hair to silky straight hair, I would fit in. Perhaps, I would feel different about being different, and I'd be more content.

Difficult though it was, I had to have straight hair. I had to get rid of my *"woolly hair"* as a girl who had begged to touch my hair had once called it.

"OO! So funny." She snatched her hand away from my hair. "Your hair feels like a sheep." She was a farmer's daughter.

I'd been told my hair was like a *Hottentot's*. I was hurt and ashamed. My hair was called, fuzzy-wuzzy and someone once said it looked like a gollywog's. Those names really hurt. I hated my hair.

I resolved to have straight hair, floppy hair. Yes, I would make my hair straight. I knew my hair would never be quite the same as the other girls, but I was determined to get it as close as possible.

It took some planning, but in the end, I worked out how to have straight hair without anyone knowing how it was achieved. It was complicated and risky, but it would be worth it in the end, as I would be like everyone else. Strange though it may be, being white wasn't something I desired. In my mind, there were some positives to being *coloured* but not enough to cancel out the major negative of my hair.

I returned to school after the summer holidays with an iron-straightening comb concealed in an old tea towel, hidden at the bottom of my soap-bag. My father had given me the heavy iron comb he'd brought back from America, where he'd visited his relatives.

It was important no one found out how I achieved my silky straight hair. I know I am going on about it, but this was important if I was to fit in. I needed a stove to heat my comb to the optimum heat, a large jar of grease, usually Vaseline and privacy. I needed somewhere private enough should I overheat the comb and burn my hair, the smell of scorched hair wouldn't be detected and cause panic. If the smell of burning started a panic and the fire brigade called it would be horrible. I shuddered at the possible humiliation. What would I say?

I gave a great deal of thought to finding a place secret enough to straighten my hair, where I wouldn't be discovered.

But where?

Boarding schools by their very nature of communal living do not offer much privacy. Sharing a dormitory with eight other girls offers no privacy. From the moment we were woken in the morning to go to Mass, we were watched over by nuns. We were never alone.

At every opportunity, I scouted around the Convent for somewhere I could straighten my hair without curious girls watching me or asking what I was doing.

I was getting desperate when eventually fate played a hand. I was lucky when the bath roster was worked out and my slot fell on Friday after tea and before supper. It meant I could wash my hair and it would be dry albeit frizzy before I went to bed. We were only allowed a bath once a week.

On the night I found the perfect place, it happened by pure chance. It had been raining hard all day, and when Sister Josephine came to collect us for bed, instead of leading us down the drive to the boarding house, as would normally happen, she led us down to the tunnel linking the main Convent house to the large boarding house. We were normally never allowed down there.

The tunnel had been built during the war (WWII) to act as a bomb shelter during air raids over the nearby town. Nuns from the main Convent building and boarders from the boarding house would congregate in the tunnel and wait out the bombing. Although not in town, there was always the possibility of a stray bomb.

The tunnel was built in such a way as to offer rooms leading off the main passage for the nuns, boarders and other people to take shelter separately.

"You don't need your Wellington boots girls. We're taking the passage."

We trooped after Sister Josephine as she led us down concrete steps next to the chapel.

I gathered my belongings and followed. The cellar was honeycombed with small rooms leading off the main underground passage and I slowed to look in all the little rooms as we passed. I stuck my head around one door after another, and it dawned me I could use one of the rooms to straighten my hair. The question was, when?

My only chance would be after midnight. Everyone would be asleep by then. Though I didn't like the idea, I couldn't think of any other opportunity.

CHAPTER 23

The nights I straightened my hair, I would force myself to stay awake until I heard the large grandfather clock on the landing chime twelve and everything was silent. I would groan softly, longing to stay in bed.

What did it matter, if I woke in the morning with a thick bush of frizz? I was at a girls' school for heaven sake, there were no boys around. It didn't matter what I looked like. But I knew having frizzy hair in the morning was not an option if I wanted to fit in.

I would glance at my sleeping roommates, open my bedside cabinet and remove my soap bag. Sister Josephine was a light sleeper, so I crept softly by her door and along the corridor to the stairs.

The wooden floors groaned and creaked as I tiptoed along the landing guided only by the silvery light of the moon shining through the tall windows. Moonless nights made the house even more creepy. There were rumours the Boarding house was haunted by a nun who'd tried to run away with her lover, the gardener's boy. She had been caught and imprisoned in a room at the top of the house many years ago. The boy she loved had been banished and as the story goes, the young nun had died mysteriously. It was said, in her grief and despair, she had taken her own life by flinging herself from the top floor bannister to the floor below. It was rumoured, her ghostly apparition, unable to rest, would wander the corridors looking for her lover.

Of course, we never found out if it had really happened. Who could say? The nuns wouldn't substantiate such a story, would they? But the very idea thrilled us, it was such a romantically sad story and the gothic design of the boarding house lent itself to the romance of forbidden love. Despite being terrified of meeting the ghost of the young nun, straightening my hair was more important to me. I squashed my fear and made my way down the stairs to the cellar. I concentrated on each step, halting each time a stair creaked. I was more frightened of waking the living, Sister Josephine, than meeting the dead.

It wasn't until I reached the bottom of the cellar steps I dared switch on my torch. The passage stretched before me. I shone my torch and crept forward, the pinprick of light disappearing into the long dark tunnel under the driveway between the boarding house and the main Convent building.

"Why do I have to do this?" Talking softly to myself gave me the illusion I wasn't alone. I somehow found it comforting.

I continued my soft monologue as I made my way through the labyrinth of tunnels and rooms. "Would it really matter if anyone knew I straightened my hair?"

I turned into a small empty damp room, the only room with a door. A door, I rationalised, could be useful to hide behind should I hear anyone coming.

Of course, I didn't expect anyone, but I could never be sure. Sister Josephine had once turned up when a group of us had crept down to the common room to have a midnight feast and had stood over us as she made us eat the cream horns we had thought would be so delicious after midnight. In the circumstances, it turned out to be quite nauseating. To this day, cream horns turn my stomach and eating at midnight has long lost its appeal.

It became the norm every Friday, when at midnight, I would creep down to the chilly little room in the tunnel under the drive of the Convent. And crouching down I would unpack my iron comb, small camping stove, methylated spirits, a jar of Vaseline and a box of matches and set about straightening my hair in my effort to be like the other girls.

I always checked and rechecked my soap-bag every Friday evening before climbing into bed. There were five essential pieces of equipment I needed and each item was as important as the other. If any of those items were missing, my excursion down to the cellar would be wasted, and my hair straightening would have to be aborted.

The small damp room in the cellar was cold, very cold. I shivered, as I hunkered down and lifted the lid of the small tin camping stove, put a match to the methylated spirits and watched as a blue flickering flame lit the room. As I placed the iron comb over the flame, I prayed I wouldn't be discovered.

I was able to buy the paraphernalia I needed, methylated spirits and matches, each Friday as after tea we were led out of the convent grounds by Sister Gerald into the small town to buy our weekly toiletries. Buying methylated spirits was my priority. I had to ensure I had enough methylated spirits for my hair straightening.

I would always position myself at the back of the crocodile line of girls, as far back as possible from Sister Gerald and peel away as we passed the hardware store. I would slip in, quickly buy a small bottle of methylated spirits and be back in line before I was missed.

A group of teddy boys with their long black velvet collar jackets, drainpipe trousers, and black suede creeper shoes, always stood idly leaning against a wall in the square, as though waiting for us, and then make suggestive comments as we walked by. We rather enjoyed the attention they gave us, despite flicking our heads dismissively and sticking our noses in the air. I made sure to cram my velour school hat firmly on my head to hide my thick bush of hair.

In the cellar at midnight, as I placed the iron comb over the flames and while waiting for it to heat, I carefully separated clumps of hair and liberally greased each section with Vaseline before pulling the hot comb through. The smell of heated Vaseline, and from time to time, the smell of scorched hair filled the little room. Should I be discovered, I would have looked like one of Shakespeare's witches bent over a cauldron cooking up an evil potion, but I couldn't even smile at the picture it conjured up. I was too cold and frightened of discovery and the sounds of movement I could hear around me, to find any of it amusing.

In the shadows, large river rats could sometimes be seen sulking in the corners, and I would have to exert stringent self-control not to scream and carry on screaming at the horror of it all. I shivered with fear each time I heard the little scurrying feet of the rats and saw their shadows, giant-like, projected onto the walls by the flickering flames of the camp stove. "They won't hurt me, they won't hurt me," I recited over and over again as my throat constricted with fear. Taking deep breaths and holding the smoking comb, my words were soft and plaintive.

Working in the dark with no mirror, meant everything was done by touch. It was no wonder there were times when the hot comb came into contact with my face leaving a scar on my temple, cheek or earlobe. The smell of charred flesh permeated the air, and I would worry the smell would bring everyone down to the cellar believing the house was on fire. I needed to make sure there was enough Vaseline on my hair to prevent burning.

There was a price to pay for straight hair, and for me, it was time spent in the dank dark cellar frequented by river rats on cold Friday nights. I so desperately wanted straight hair, sacrificing my sleep, squashing my fears of the horrors of the dark cold cellar and the possible threat of discovery, was a small price to pay

The ritual of heating the comb, testing it on the old tea towel, letting it cool down a little if it scorched the cloth, combing it through the portion of prepared hair, was honed to a skill by the time I left school.

CHAPTER 24

My clandestine hair straightening sessions in the cellar continued until the river running alongside the school and under the drive burst its banks and flooded the school.

The cellar was knee deep in water and unusable. I became anxious. The door to the cellar was padlocked and there was no way I could use it.

I did a reconnaissance of the whole convent and grounds knowing I had to find a new secret place, a place where no one would come looking for me.

I slipped away after lunch soon after the flood and wandered through the apple orchard brooding about my predicament. It seemed impossible that I would find a place as private and as safe as the cellar to straighten my hair. The cellar being out of commission was a major set back.

The apple orchard ran down to the river and was out of bounds, which was reassuring, as it meant no one would be around. I spent some time sitting on the riverbank under a large weeping willow, feeling sorry for myself. I watched a large river rat swimming downstream and shuddered remembering the rats in the cellar.

On the way back to class, I stumbled across an old wooden hut I hadn't noticed before. It was in a dilapidated, broken down condition and looked abandoned. The wood was cracked and splintered.

I pushed open the wooden door and gingerly stepped in to find myself in a small dusty and empty space save for a few rusting garden tools. My heart skipped a beat. Perfect. It was unlikely anyone would come this way, except of course Joe the gardener and by the state of the tools, I doubted he still used them. The old wooden hut would be a safe place to straighten my hair.

The idea of creeping out of the boarding house at midnight set my heart beating with anxiety. Nuns prayed at such odd times, I wouldn't be able to use my torch, in case it was seen from one of the convent windows.

It would make sense therefore, if I waited until all the nuns went to the chapel for morning prayers at five. It was then, I could slip down to the shed unseen. It was risky but workable. If I worked fast, I could straighten my hair and be back in bed by the time the nuns' prayers were over.

From then on, I rose on Saturday mornings and as soon as I heard Sister Josephine leave the boarding house. I would wait until I heard the back door shut and then swing my legs out of bed, dress quickly and creep down the stairs, out the back door, skirt the swimming pool, round the tennis courts and on towards the orchard.

As I set out the camping stove, I knew I'd never return to the cellar, this hut was perfect. I did wonder what I would say if inadvertently a stray spark set fire to the splintered timber shed.

It never failed to amaze me how on Saturday morning when we were all gathered at breakfast, no one mentioned the difference in my hair from the night before. Would they think the transformation from crinkly frizz to greasy straight overnight was miraculous? Perhaps they hadn't noticed or weren't bothered. Still, I felt my hair needed to be straight if I had any chance of being the same as everyone else.

Damp weather was my nemesis, as my sleek greasy hair would immediately revert to its natural frizz should anything wet touch it. This was a major difficulty since I lived in the northern hemisphere.

However, every Saturday morning I prayed it wouldn't rain and somehow my prayers were answered.

Everything went well for a few weeks, until one Saturday after breakfast I had a message from Sister Theresa that she wanted to see me. I thought nothing of her summons as I hurried to the laundry outbuilding. Perhaps, I thought, my school blouse was extra dirty and she wanted to warn me about being so mucky.

"Harmony," she said as I entered the laundry. She was struggling to fold a sheet, and I went to help her.

"You said you wanted to see me, Sister," I said matching one corner of the sheet to the other corner, shaking it in unison with her and moving forward to join my end to hers.

"I wanted to ask you about what you were doing this morning?"

I gave her a puzzled look.

"I saw you coming from the orchard."

There were many positives as well as negatives to being a Catholic. One positive is learning very early, how to lie. I had to develop the skill of thinking on my feet, along with honing a look of total innocence when questioned or accused of anything.

"Yes, Sister." I sighed and tried for an expression of piety. "I woke up early (truth) and didn't want to wake the other girls (truth), and so thought I'd go for a walk to the apple orchard (half-truth) to say my rosary (a big, big lie)."

Sister Theresa looked momentarily surprised and then smiled, her eyes lit up, her round pink cheeks dimpling as her smile broadened. "Harmony, you could have joined us in the chapel."

"Thank you, Sister," I said helping her fold another sheet. "But I often like to be alone, when I say the rosary."

She nodded as though she understood the need for solitude and I felt a momentary flash of compassion for her. Imagine having to spend her life with a bunch of women? Most likely the only real peace she got was when silence was imposed on them after nine in the evenings.

"I suppose it's alright then." She picked up a basket of wet clothes and hurried into the yard. I followed with the bag of wooden pegs.

"Don't forget Harmony." She paused as she hung a bra. "You can always join us in the chapel."

"Yes, Sister." I gave her pegs until she had finished hanging all the clothes, our blouses, bras, vest and knickers. She brought out another basket containing white materials, their nuns' wimples and I suspected other articles of nuns wear. She saw the curiosity on my face.

"Thank you for your help, Harmony," she said. "You can go now."

I left happy with the outcome. Should any other nun ever see me going or coming from the orchard in future, Sister Theresa would reassure them I was only seeking solitude to say the Rosary.

CHAPTER 25

Before starting College I took a holiday job at a hotel in Dorset. My parents weren't happy I was going to be out of their supervision for three whole months and I suspected my father thought I might return home pregnant. Such was his suspicion of all men and lack of trust in me.

I applied in writing for the job, advertised in 'The Lady' magazine, and having been accepted panicked. Suppose I turned up and the owner, seeing I was *coloured*, told me the job was no longer mine? What would I do?

I decided to phone her, rather than write. In that way, she would have to say she didn't want me. She may have difficulty showing her prejudice, voice to voice.

"Thank you for offering me the holiday job in your hotel," I said when she picked up the phone.

"It's okay," she replied. "This is a busy time of year, so we're looking forward to having extra hands helping us out."

"By the way," I added trying to sound casual, though my stomach clenched and unclenched with nervousness. Suppose she said, she didn't want me? "You ought to know," I continued. "I'm not white."

"I see."

I held my breath as a heartbeat of hesitation stretched before us.

"Well come down anyway."

Later, when we got to know each other, she told me, she had been afraid her guests may object, but she was so short handed, she was desperate and didn't have time to advertise again. Besides, she'd said, my accent was very English and it convinced her I would fit in. So I got the job. In the end, only one of her guests objected in the three months I worked at the hotel and Mrs Carter protected me and never let me clean that guest's room or serve her table in the restaurant.

Why oh why, I thought, did I always have to be aware what people would think if they knew I wasn't white? But I was afraid of the hostility and rejection I may face based on the colour of my skin. If people knew what they were getting, knew I wasn't white, there may be a chance I would be judged on my abilities, my attributes rather than their preconceived ideas of *coloured* people. Why did I always have to think of my colour? It seemed to me, I always had to apologies for the colour of my skin. The world seemed so unfair. Would there ever be a time when it didn't matter?

I phoned David, the boy next door. You remember, the boy I used to play spies with and chase birds around the garden with a cone of Saxa salt? He had moved away, but we were friends and always kept in touch.

"I'll drive you down to Dorset," he said. "I've just passed my driving test and could do with driving a long journey."

David and I had been friends since I was eight, and he a year older. Even during the *'hate the other sex,'* stage of development, we remained friends. And now we would talk frequently, telling each other of our plans and dreams.

On the way down to Dorset, he expressed his concern. "You will be so far away from home. If anything goes wrong, promise you will phone me and I will come and collect you."

I smiled at him. "Don't worry. What could possibly go wrong?"

"If it does, phone me. Promise. If you're okay, I come and collect you when it's time for you to go home."

I turned to look at him and for the first time saw him as the blond, blue-eyed, good looking-man he'd grown into. He'd always been David, my friend. It was a shame I wasn't attracted to him, but he was just my playmate. And I knew he felt the same about me.

When we arrived at the hotel, I noticed the way the Mrs Carter looked at David. She asked me later if he was my boyfriend and was surprised when I said, he was only a friend. Looking back at her reaction, she must have seen something I hadn't noticed.

It was after my wedding, I learned how David felt about me. He phoned me after I had returned from my honeymoon. I was excited to tell him about the wonderful places Barry, and I had visited.

He forestalled me. "I never thought you would marry someone who wasn't coloured. If I'd thought you would marry someone white, I would..." He never finished his sentence.

That was the last time we spoke to each other. And to this day I still feel an immense sadness that my being coloured, prevented David from declaring how he felt about me. He'd kept silent out of fear. Had he'd told me how he'd felt, he feared, he would lose our friendship.

Of course in the midst of all of this, there remained the issue of my hair. I believed the straighter my hair, the more I would fit in. I'd packed my camping stove, my straightening comb, my Vaseline and matches. In my little room off the kitchen, after everyone had gone to bed and the hotel was quiet, I would set up my equipment and straighten my hair.

It was summer and the hotel was busy. My job was fairly simple. All I had to do was serve breakfast, lunch and dinner and clean the guest bedrooms, bathrooms and toilets. Between lunch and dinner, I was free to do as I wished.

After lunch, I would put on my bikini, slip on my sundress, grab a towel and a book and make for the beach. I loved the sun and sand and I loved my tiny green bikini. The beach was large, and I was able to find a quiet spot amongst the sand dunes to soak up the sun and read.

Of course, I had to go to Mass on Sunday, my mother had made sure to remind me before I left home that missing Mass would be a mortal sin. In order to make up the time missed when I should have been serving breakfast, it was agreed I would serve tea every Sunday.

Generally, the guests were friendly and polite towards me, although I did rather dread going into room number seven. The occupant always made sure to be there while I cleaned his room. He would sit by the window his eyes following me around the room as I made up the bed, and tidied and dusted. His wife was never there and as soon as I had finished, I would see him leave and make his way down to the beach. It was rather strange the way he watched me, he may have thought I was going to steal his belongings. I was frightened of him. But I couldn't tell anyone since he hadn't done anything, and Mrs Carter may believe it was my imagination. Mrs Carter wouldn't want to upset her guest, and I was only a chambermaid and waitress, for goodness sake. Who would she believe if there were any complaints? I didn't have any confidence a *coloured* chambermaid would be believed over a paying guest.

I asked Mrs Carter about him. "The man in room seven," I said casually one morning when I was serving breakfast and had returned for more toast.

"You mean Mr Webster?"

"Yes, Mr Webster."

"He and his wife come every summer. Is he worrying you? He was rather curious about you. He was asking me about you the other day," she said taking the cigarette out of her mouth and flicking the ash into the overflowing ashtray next to the toaster.

She'd moved on to another subject when I returned with an order for fried eggs, bacon, fried bread and black pudding, and I didn't get a chance to return to the subject of Mr Webster's curiosity about me.

I bore Mr Webster's presence each morning for the remainder of his two weeks. Each time I cleaned his room, I made sure to leave the door open and always greet him politely.

To my surprise, he presented me with a large box of chocolates on his last morning. "Thought you may like these," he said shyly. "In appreciation of all, you have done to make our stay here very comfortable."

I accepted the chocolates, feeling the heat rise in my face and thanked him.

When I showed the chocolates to Mrs. Carter, she laughed.

"Well," she said. "Mr Webster really took a shine to you."

My discomfort with Mr Webster resurfaced. His behaviour had been unusual, but I took comfort he'd be gone the next day.

CHAPTER 26

It was a gloriously hot sunny day on my first Sunday in Dorset. As I stood at the bus stop waiting for the bus into Swanage, I was happy. The hotel stood on top of cliffs looking out to sea, offering a wonderful view. Dorset was beautiful. Everything had worked out well, in fact, more than well.

A motorbike sped by, stopped, and turned. I stepped back wondering what the rider wanted. There were no other cars on the road. I was totally alone. The rider had sandy hair and hazel eyes and as he drew up next to me he gave a wide friendly grin.

"Are you going to Swanage?"

"Yes." I nodded.

"Can I give you a lift? I think you've missed the bus."

"No thank you."

"Come on. I won't bite you," he said. "Hop on the back. You'll be quite safe."

I had no idea when the next bus was due, perhaps not for hours. Not wanting to miss Mass and not wanting to be seen returning to the hotel, when I'd asked for the time to go to church, I climbed gingerly on the pillion seat.

"My name's Adrian," he said gunning the engine. "And you?"

"Harmony," I said.

"Well, Harmony, wrap your arms around me and let's be off."

I told him where I wanted to go and he laughed. "Catholic eh?"

We took off at speed, and I gripped him tightly around his waist. It was my first experience of riding pillion on a motorbike and it was both terrifying and exhilarating.

He asked if he could pick me up after Mass and was waiting for me revving his engine as I stepped back out of the church into the sunlight.

"How about a walk on the beach?" He asked as I climbed again onto the pillion seat.

I agreed, and for the next four weeks we met at the bus stop every Sunday and he dropped me off at church. He would wait and pick me up after mass. I thought he was nice. Adrian was interesting to talk to, he made me laugh and we never seemed to be short of things to say to each other.

On the fifth week, everything changed. We went for a walk on the beach as usual after Mass and he walked towards some rather large sand dunes.

"Let's sit here," he said and pulled me down into a particularly deep rut between two sand dunes.

I sat and he started kissing me. We'd kissed before, nothing too passionate, just pleasant. But this time it was different. He was rough and demanding as he pushed his tongue hard into my mouth. His hands gripped my shoulders, and he pushed me roughly down onto the sand. The stubble of dune grass stuck into to my back hurting me through my sundress, and I gasped in pain.

"This is how you like it isn't it?" he said in a harsh cruel voice.

"Let me go."

He laughed. It was a laugh I'd never heard from him before. It was as though he was a stranger.

"No," I gasped. "Let me go." I struggled and pushed against rough hands now moving down my body. I pushed hard against his body as his hand reached my hemline and started to scrunch my dress up to my thighs. His lips crushed against mine, I managed to free my lips, turning my face away and gasped, "Let me go. Please stop." I felt violated and dirty. I had to get him off me. The more I kicked, and struggled, the more he fought against me and seemed to enjoy it.

"I'll scream," I threatened, and he went slack momentarily. I took my opportunity and bit him. I sank my teeth deep into his shoulder and clamped my jaw shut. He screamed and leapt up and away from me.

"You bitch," he snarled.

"Leave me alone." I gasped struggling to stand and push my skirt down.

"You people," he sneered. "Who do you think you are?"

I scrambled to my feet brushing sand off my dress. I was terrified he was going to hit me. His face was suffused with red blotches, his lips drawn back and his eyes blazed with fury as he spat the words at me.

I cowered back and looked around for a quick escape route away from him.

I was too frightened to feel angry. Had I led him on? Was it my fault?

"I wouldn't touch you if you paid me, nigger."

He turned and walked away striding over the sand dunes towards the road and his motorbike.

I had plenty of time to castigate myself for getting into such a situation. I was stupid for believing Adrian liked me as a person when in truth, he thought he could do what he liked with me. In his eyes, I was a nigger. When I rebuffed him, his pride was hurt and his true feelings about me were revealed.

Chastened, I walked the three miles back to the hotel in the heat of the day and arrived in time to serve tea. I desperately wanted to bathe, to wash any tactile memory of Adrian off me. But I had to serve tea, so slipped on my blue overall and walked into the small lounge to take orders for tea. My experience with Adrian had left me with a feeling I was in some way to blame for the whole incident. A feeling of déjà vu swept over me and once more, the spectra of Mr O'Neal hung over me and crept into my memory yet again. Would I ever get over what happened to me at school when I was only ten?

CHAPTER 27

Going to college would be another milestone in my life. Naturally, it was an all-female Teacher Training College. Still, I was happy because it was an opportunity to become a student and to be treated as an adult. Surely I would be in a world where being *coloured* didn't matter.

A nun met me when I arrived. I shuddered when unsmilingly she greeted me. "You must be Harmony Brown," she said. Her lips cracked into an unconvincing smile. "Welcome."

She was dressed in the same habit as Sister Agatha, I shuddered, she belonged to the same order of nuns and spoke with the same accent. I had a sense of foreboding but shook it away. What could she do to me? I was a grown-up now.

"My name is Sister Margaret," she told me as she led me across the quadrangle to the student hostel I would be living in for the year.

"All our first-year students share rooms," she said as she led the way upstairs and pushed open a door marked six. "And we make sure to put each girl with another girl from the same town or area of the country."

As the door swung open a black girl who'd been standing looking out of the window turned to look at us. Surprise showed on her face as her eyes fell on me.

"This is your room-mate Clara," Sister Margaret said giving the staring girl a fleeting smile. "This is Harmony, Clara, I'm sure you'll both get on well together as you will find you both have a lot in common."

Clara took a step away from the window and faced Sister Margaret. She drew herself up and looked at Sister Margaret with an expression of scorn. "Like what?" she asked.

"Well Clara," Sister Margaret gave her a condescending smile as though Clara had missed the point entirely. "Well...," there was a momentary hesitation. "You're both from the same country."

"And what country is that?" Clara asked, her back stiffening as her eyes swept over Sister Margaret with unabashed contempt.

"You both come from Africa."

Clara's eyes blazed as she turned to me. "Where do you come from?" she demanded.

I was caught off guard and almost missed her question. I had been fascinated watching someone *coloured* take on the clear prejudice of another.

I became aware of two pairs of eyes watching me.

"Oh!" I gasped. "I live in London, though I was born in Coventry. But my mother does..."

Clara cut me off, a note of satisfaction in her voice. "London is hardly Africa."

She turned and faced Sister Margaret triumphantly. "And if she did come from Africa, I would bet it wouldn't be the same country in Africa as I come from."

"Clara!" Sister Margaret gasped.

Clara hadn't finished. "You assumed because we aren't white, we both come from Africa and that Africa is a country. If I said, Germany, France and Ireland are the same country would you would agree? Would you agree if I said you were German because you come from Europe? After all, you are all from Europe and all white."

"You are being ridiculous Clara," Sister Margaret faltered backing towards the door. "You're being far too touchy."

"The real reason Harmony and I are sharing the same room, is because we are both black, isn't it?"

Sister Margaret heaved up her ample bosom and turned, her white wimple accentuated the rise in the colour of her cheeks as marched towards the door. She shut the door with a resounding bang, but not before turning to glare at both of us with a look of undisguised dislike, adding, "Make sure you are both ready for supper in half an hour."

As the door closed, Clara threw herself back on her bed and laughed. "Hopefully, she will stay away from us now."

I sat on my bed and looked at the first *coloured girl* I had ever come into close contact with. "Incredible." I breathed with admiration. "I wouldn't have dared."

"Yes, you would," Clara said sitting up to look at me. " You would have dared if you'd had to face all the prejudice I have."

But I'd had been through endless prejudice, and more, though I said nothing to Clara. Much of my experiences were still too painful to talk about.

I learned Clara came from a very wealthy influential family from a country on the West Coast of Africa. She had spent many years in an English boarding school and the last two years had been in Switzerland at a finishing school. She had returned home every holiday and so was able to replenish her identity as a black African. She had little tolerance for people who were prejudiced against us, and never missed an opportunity to point it out.

We became good friends and our friendship lasted many years until we lost touch when her country was thrown into the chaos of a coup, a war of genocide and the total destruction and dislocation that followed.

Clara never straightened her hair, she plaited it in tight neat rows. She looked wonderful, startlingly beautiful. She never dated and avoided going out to meet people. "I don't like white men." She once told me. "Because they're white, they think they can treat us as prostitutes. They immediately fall into a colonialist mindset in the presence of black women."

I was horrified.

"Besides I have enough of dating, when I go home," she said one day as she watched me getting ready to go out on a date. "There are no black boys here. And I like men, not stupid immature white boys."

CHAPTER 28

I was prepared for college in a way only people afraid of not being accepted by the society in which they lived would prepare a daughter. It was important I fitted in. Both my mother and father feared I would somehow shame them if out of their sphere of control.

"Don't get involved with any West Indians," my father advised.

My eyes widened in puzzlement. Wasn't my father a West Indian?

"They're not to be trusted," he added. "They can't be faithful."

Was he talking about himself?

"Also, white men are no better." He looked worried. "You have to remember, white men, see *coloured* girls as easy, hot, exotic and earthy. They're only interested in getting you into bed as quickly as possible. They will boast to their friends they've had a *coloured* girl, then marry one of their own."

I should add here, I did date someone who once remarked I was '*earthy*'. It was only once because I never dated him again. It may have been a compliment, but I wasn't prepared to take the risk.

On the occasion of my father's remarks about boyfriends, memories of my experience with Adrian in Dorset sent a shudder through me. Basically, my father didn't want me to meet or go out with anyone of the opposite sex.

To complicate matters, my mother had different guidelines. She advised I didn't go out with Nigerians. Her rationale being, "They're too argumentative. And our relatives in Ghana wouldn't like it."

My head whirled with confusion. My parents were against, just about every ethnic group, or any religion that was different. Most importantly, all males were unacceptable. Worst of all, having suffered from prejudice themselves, my parents were prejudiced against others. It didn't make sense.

Sister Agatha came to mind. She had blamed the Jews for the crucifixion of Jesus Christ and the whole race, in her opinion, were condemned to everlasting punishment. Then, of course, I mustn't forget Reverend Mother's warning that men over thirty should be avoided at all cost.

They were all, however, in agreement with one thing, I must never, ever, countenance, a man who was not Catholic.

Was there anyone left?

Lecherous men were not the only concern my father voiced. "You need to be better than all the white people around you," he had said a few days before I left for college. "Remember they have expectations of what coloured people are like. So you have to be twice as good, at everything you do. And never forget what white men think of *coloured* women."

I shrugged off his comments. College would be different. Surely educated people wouldn't be *that* prejudiced?

I would have thought, the lecturers at the college, training us to be teachers, would have been aware of, and against stereotyping. But not so.

I was made intensely aware I was different very early on. A lecturer instructing us how to teach mathematics to children under ten, whilst demonstrating a new method for teaching long division, turned to us and said, "Remember, the nigger in the woodpile is..." he stopped momentarily, looked at me briefly and then continued. There were a few titters from the other students. I was excruciatingly embarrassed, aware all eyes were on me. I sat in the middle of the group wishing the floor would open up and swallow me. Was it possible, I was the only one feeling any discomfort?

I wished Clara had been in the lecture with me. I am sure she would have had something to say. But I was too timid, too aware that I was alone and so, not wanting to rock the boat, kept silent.

During my three-year stint at college, there were many instances of offensive comments about us nonwhites. And those remarks were made by people preparing us to teach the future generation. If I objected I would have been accused of being too sensitive. The expression used in those days, if *coloured* people took umbrage would be, they *'had a chip on their shoulder'* about not being white. I didn't want to be seen as having a *'chip on my shoulder'*.

I longed to be accepted. I wanted to be accepted for what I was. I tried everything I could think of to be accepted. But still, I always knew wasn't.

A lecturer I didn't like because of the way he used to look at me in lectures was heard saying to another lecturer, as they'd both watched me walk across the quadrangle, "just look at her. She's a sexy bitch. But what do you expect from these people?"

I wasn't flattered when his words were repeated to me. I was appalled. I was upset to be casually called, a sexy bitch. It was unbelievably discriminatory. I wasn't a bitch and neither was I sexy, at least not deliberately. *Sexy* was his interpretation...his thoughts of me. And what had he meant by *'these people'*?

There was more to me than that.

After hearing how I'd been described, I always chose to go to my lectures by another more roundabout route, so as not to pass the staffroom window.

He was a man who thought it acceptable to abuse me verbally to another person, based solely on my being, a *coloured* woman. Did he make such openly crude comments about any of the other female students? Somehow, I had my doubts.

I felt it was the most painful thing said about me, whilst I was at college.

What did I have to do no to incite such crude comments?

Being coloured in a white world was, I found, endlessly wearisome and sometimes utterly painful.

CHAPTER 29

The world, according to my parents, was crammed with men deemed to be unsuitable and dangerous. All men were only after one thing, sex, and my job was to make sure they didn't succeed with me. I was to be eternally vigilant where any man was concerned.

On top of their instilled fears of the evil intentions of men, for which I had to be constantly wary, there was the unspoken pressure to find a husband before I was left on the shelf. If Reverend Mother's warning about men in their thirties, was something to be worried about, what would she have said about single women in their thirties? It would be unthinkable. I had to find a husband, at least get one lined up, and as soon as possible.

Finding a husband had turned out to be much more complicated than anyone could imagine. My choices, it appeared, were abysmally limited.

But I was determined not to give up. It was then, I decided my future husband had to be white. I wouldn't put my children through what I had been through simply because I was *coloured*. I would find a man who would make a faithful, loyal, responsible husband, someone prepared to have lots of children, since being a Catholic meant contraception was not allowed.

In hindsight, it was an incredibly hard goal to achieve. But I remained positive and determined not to be daunted by the task I faced. I would look for someone capable of taking care of me, and the children I wanted to have. I would look for someone to provide me with the lifestyle I expected and someone my parents would see as marginally suitable. Not, I hoped too impossible a task, despite my parents' dire warnings about men.

Surely I would know what was right for me.

My first boyfriend at college was Jeff. I met him at a college Hop, nowadays called a disco. We danced all evening, and he asked me out. I was flattered but realised as soon as we had been out on a few dates something was missing.

It was when he told me he'd had a breakdown a year before we'd met and had gone on to divulge that voices from the radio had told him what to do that I began to feel concerned. But when he confessed he sometimes wished for a rifle and would like to climb up to the top of a church tower and pick people *off* from the street below that my anxiety grew exponentially. He blamed his break-down on the stress of the up and coming exams and assured me, as long as he didn't forget to take his drugs, all would be well. I'd nodded and made sympathetic noises. How dreadful for him, I sympathised. But realistically, I recognised he was not husband material.

Fearing I may cause lasting harm if I broke up with him when he first told me about his breakdown, I dated him until he'd finished his final exams.

I never met his mother, because, he told me, she'd be too shocked I wasn't white. He didn't want to upset her further, not after the distress his breakdown had caused.

"She gets easily upset," he'd once said when his mother was to visit him and he couldn't see me that weekend.

My next boyfriend was wonderful, down to earth and fun. He was gentle and sweet and professed to love me a great deal, and because he was such a warm loving, open person, I fell in love with him. The only problem being, he had a mother who hated me on sight.

We met during my first year of teaching and as the year wore on, we talked about spending our lives together. That was until I met his mother; a tall thin, aspiring middle-class woman who made no effort to hide her instant dislike of me.

I was taken to tea.

"How do you do Harmony?" There was a parody of a smile on her thin lips as we were introduced. We briefly brushed hands, then she spun on her heels and headed for the kitchen saying, "I could do with your help, Peter."

Amidst the rattling of cups and plates, low angry voices could be heard coming from the kitchen. Peter's father, a kind man, talked politely to me about my journey up to see them. And when our conversation dried up, we struggled to find something to say to each other. We were painfully aware something unpalatable was taking place a few feet away. The angry voices coming from the kitchen were difficult to ignore, and we were both embarrassed.

After her greeting, not once during the few hours of my visit, did Maggie Miller speak directly to me. Any questions or comments she made were directed to me, through her son.

She had set the table as though she was about to produce a banquet, with numerous spoons, knives and pastry forks stretching into infinity. It was tea, four O'clock in the afternoon tea, for heaven sake!

Luckily my socially conscious mother had schooled me in the refinements of table etiquette such as place settings. Therefore, I wasn't in anyway intimidated.

"Ask Harmony if she would like more tea," she said at one point, and added later, "Peter, is Harmony warm enough?"

It was the middle of June and a typical English summer day, a very pleasant, June day.

Maggie Miller sat at the head of the table, her husband on her right and Peter on her left. When she looked at me, her face was hard with suppressed anger and dislike.

Maggie Miller was conspicuous by her absence as we said good-bye, for which I was grateful. I heard a door slam from deep within the house and caught a look pass between Peter and his father.

Maggie Miller had reacted as though I was a specimen so foreign to civilized society, direct contact had to be avoided, at all costs.

I knew then my relationship with Peter was doomed. Maggie Miller would come between us at every opportunity and would continue to do so if Peter and I married. Rather than let Peter's mother destroy our relationship in the future, I gave him up. I did what I believed I had to do and in the process, I broke my heart.

"It's no good," I told him after our visit to his parents. "Your mother will never accept I'm not white. Family is important to me, and I'm not spending my life fighting your mother for you."

Peter hadn't argued, it was a though he knew by being the only son, the only child, his mother would never fully let him go. As I cried myself to sleep that night, I knew Maggie Miller would be happy with the knowledge her son was safe.

CHAPTER 30

I returned home after spending a year teaching in Southern England and moved back home. My heart was broken and sympathetic though they were, I suspected my parents were secretly pleased since my mother was quick to point out men were not worth any heartache. I knew if I'd been white, Peter and I would still be together.

I decided I would become a nun. By becoming a nun, I would take myself out of the marriage marketplace and best of all, I wouldn't feel compelled to look for a suitable husband. I was saddened at the thought of never having children but accepted it was the price of being *coloured*. Besides, I had been very happy at my Convent boarding school and never once experienced any real prejudice.

It was a warm June evening and when I walked down the drive of my old Convent school, I felt a tinge of sadness as I was no longer the blossoming eager teenager I had once been. I remembered my longing to get out into the world and throw myself into all the possibilities out there, career, dates, men, parties and goodness knows what else. In four short years, my bubble of excitement had been burst. I wanted to feel safe again. The world was an unkind place, and I didn't want anything to do with it. God wouldn't turn me down because of the *colour* of my skin, surely?

"Harmony, my dear," Reverend Mother said as we sat in the parlour. "It's really nice of you to come back and visit us."

Sister Margaret Mary brought in a tray of tea and rock cakes, my favourite when at school.

"Harmony, it's lovely to see you. Things have not been the same since you left school?" She laughed as she greeted me, handed me a tea plate and placed a cup and saucer next to me. Reverend Mother smiled.

"Have you finished your teacher training course now?" Reverend Mother asked when we were alone.

I nodded.

"Have you got a post yet?"

I told her about my first year of teaching and now my move back to London and the small Catholic school I would be teaching in for the coming year. I made no mention of Peter or my heartbreak.

"Reverend Mother," I began. "I've come to ask your permission to enter." The word, *enter*, was a euphemism for becoming a nun, joining the Convent.

"Is that what you really want my dear?" She gave me a penetrating look over the top of her half-moon glasses.

"Yes, Reverend Mother, I've been thinking about it for quite awhile now," I lied. If I confessed I was looking for a way out of life's constant struggle to fit into the society I was born into, and the struggle to find a husband, she would turn me down there and then.

She sighed. "Harmony, many are called but few are chosen." She gave me another penetrating look. "I want you to think seriously about your wish to join us. The religious life is very hard. It is a great sacrifice. It would mean giving up all worldly things that bring joy in this world. There would be no intimate relationship with another person and as such, you would feel very lonely at times. There would be no children in your life. Instead, you would look after other people's children, never your own. You would be dedicating your life to the vows of poverty, chastity and obedience. Are you prepared for all the things you would have to give up?"

My heart sank. No, I hadn't thought about religious life in the way Reverend Mother had portrayed. She made it sound unappealing, very unappealing. I thought of Peter and the pain I still felt at not having him in my life. The upside of being a nun would be no more heartbreak and therefore, no more pain. Yes, I was ready to give up the pain of heartbreak and never having to think about what being *coloured* would mean to my life.

"Yes Reverend Mother," I replied. "I am prepared for all it involves, to be part of the religious life and dedicate myself to Christ."

She nodded. "All right my child. I will agree to you joining us on one condition."

"Anything Reverend Mother," I said quickly before I changed my mind.

"I want you to work for a year at the school you have contracted to work at and during that time, I want you to go out and lead a normal life, meeting people and doing all the things young people of your age do."

I gasped in astonishment. I would have thought they would have been grateful to have young women eager to become nuns, particularly someone like me qualified to teach in one of their Convent schools. But I had to agree to Reverend Mother's terms. A year seemed a long time to be buffeted by the slights of prejudice and blatant hostility simply because of my colour. But if I had to accept Reverend Mother's conditions to prove my vocation, I had no choice. Besides, one of the three major vows was, obedience. Was Reverend Mother testing me?

"Yes Reverend Mother," I acquiesced with a nod of my head. I would spend the year preparing for my new life as a Bride of Christ. I vowed silently to go to Mass daily and even offer to teach Catechism in the church hall on Saturdays. And when the time came for me to enter, I would be the kindest most loving nun on this earth. Perhaps I would get sent to the missions to help black babies.

We stood on the doorstep of the Convent saying goodbye to one another and Reverend Mother took both my hands in hers.

"God bless you, my dear," she said softly, her eyes slightly damp. "Come and visit us often during this year, so we can see how you are getting on."

Father Jerome arrived as I turned to leave. "Hello, Harmony. How nice to see you. Are you staying long?"

"No Father, I'm leaving now. I have a train to catch."

"It's a good thing I turned up," he said smiling kindly. "I can drop you at the station. I'm going to visit a sick parishioner."

Reverend Mother beamed. "It would be very kind of you, Father."

"Thank you, Father," I said. The very last thing I wanted was to spend any time in the company of Father Jerome. He was the father confessor of the Convent and lived in the small house near the chapel. Around him I always felt uncomfortable, not withstanding he had listened to my sins every Saturday for several years. Even when I tried to disguise my voice, he always recognised me. Most of all, I recalled the time poor Bernice Elliot, on his instruction, had to confess she had insulted him by calling him Jerome without the preface of, Father.

Bernice, I remembered, was known to us girls as Miss *Malaprop*, and she had gone to confession the following Saturday and said, "Bless me father for I have sinned…this week I assaulted a Priest." It caused great mirth when she told us and I remember Reverend Mother taking Bernice aside for a quiet word, most likely to explain the difference between the words *insult* and *assault*.

Now faced with Father Jerome's offer to take me to the station and with Reverend Mother smiling on benevolently, I had no choice but to climb into his small Ford car and wave as I was driven out of the Convent grounds.

"I plan to go to London next week," Father Jerome said as we turned into the station forecourt.

"How nice," I murmured as he applied the brakes. I reached for the door handle desperate to get away as fast as I could.

"Wait, Harmony." He placed a hand on my arm. "The train isn't due yet. I'd like it if you stayed and we chatted for a while."

I couldn't think of anything worse, but I nodded, "Yes, Father."

"I would like us to meet while I'm in London. I don't know anyone there, and it would be nice to meet someone who knows the place."

"Yes, Father." I couldn't say *no* to a priest. Good Catholic girls didn't say no to a man of the cloth, though I hated the very idea of meeting him in London. He took hold of my hand and gave it a quick squeeze. Shocked I jerked it away and picked up my handbag.

"Give me your phone number. I'll give you a ring when I get to London and we can arrange to meet."

I scribbled down my number, said a quick goodbye, scrambled out of the car and ran onto the platform.

CHAPTER 31

I knew my parents would be happy with my decision to enter a religious order, particularly as Father Keenan, our Parish priest, had said, having a son or daughter enter the religious life, would bring a hundredfold of blessings. Father Keenan never clarified the kind of blessings my mother would receive. She was delighted at the thought of countless blessings.

"I'm so unlucky when it comes to men," I said at breakfast one morning after my meeting with Reverend Mother and my request to join their order of nuns.

My father's way of consoling me was to repeat one of his edicts, "bad luck is better than no luck at all."

How helpful was that?

On hearing I had decided to become a nun, he smiled with relief and said. "What better son-in-law could a father have than, Jesus Christ himself?"

My mother nodded benignly in agreement, no doubt thinking of the hundredfold of rewards she would receive for giving her daughter to Jesus Christ.

Father Jerome phoned a week later and as my mother greeted him and handed the phone to me, I screwed up my face in disgust and racked my brain desperately for any scenario I could dream up to prevent me from meeting him. I couldn't say my mother was ill since she had just spoken to him and sounded in the pink of health.

What would happen if I said I'd sprained my ankle? I had horrifying visions of Father Jerome feeling compelled to visit me, and my mother fawningly inviting him in. Besides, she wouldn't lie, certainly not to a priest.

I accepted the inevitable and said, "Hello Father."

"I trust you are well Harmony," he said formally.

"Yes, Father." I'd blown any opportunity of pleading ill health.

"I hope you don't mind," he continued sounding surprisingly unsure of himself, "but I booked some seats to go and see a new film, *West Side Story*. I would have booked a play, but priests aren't supposed to be seen going to the theatre."

Why weren't priests allowed to go to the theatre? I felt sorry for him. Of course, I'd keep him company going to the cinema.

We arranged to meet at Victoria Station. "I would like to take you out to dinner afterwards," he said. "I won't have had time to eat before I meet you."

He pulled at my heartstrings again. Priests have such a raw deal. Imagine not having dinner before he came out. I knew he was staying at the presbytery of a priest who was Father confessor at a Convent in London. Of course I would have dinner with him. How could I say no?

As I got ready to meet him, my mother slipped into my room and sat on the end of my bed.

"It will be nice to go out with Father Jerome at least I know he won't make a pass at me," I said trying to convince myself there were some positive to going out with my Father confessor. I pushed the memory of our last meeting, the station hand holding incident, out of my mind, telling myself it was nothing, he was just being nice.

"You'll be able to relax and enjoy the outing. You don't have to worry about being home on time. We know you will be safe with Father Jerome."

Life is strange, the one evening I hoped to end my outing with

Father Jerome and get home early, was the very evening my mother gave me an extension of my curfew.

When we met, I was surprised to see Father Jerome without his priest's collar. In fact, he didn't look like a priest at all. He wore a blue blazer and underneath, a pale blue shirt. His trousers were dark gray and his shoes though black looked new and casual. Looking at him, it would be impossible to guess he was a priest.

He enjoyed the film and so did I. Over dinner we discussed gang life in America and how sad it was some people couldn't have the relationship they wanted with the people they loved because of prejudice of one sort or another. I thought of Peter and wondered what he was doing now? I remembered how he'd held me and told me he'd loved me, but not enough obviously, as he hadn't been in touch. I pushed back thoughts of Peter and sighed.

"Would you like something else?" Father Jerome asked as our plates were removed.

"Just a coffee please."

He ordered and as the waitress moved away bent towards me and took hold of my hand. "You have such beautiful hands," he said tenderly wrapping my hand in his. His thumb gently stroked the back of my hand. "And so soft," he murmured as though in wonder.

Embarrassed I tried to pull my hand away.

"No don't," he said softly. "I want to ask you a question and I want you to answer me honestly."

My breath caught in my throat. Answer honestly? Didn't he remember the lies I'd had to confess? "Yes, of course, I will, Father." I let a smile touch my lips and yet felt guilty.

He drew in a deep breath and lowered his voice. "What do you think of me, Harmony?"

What could I say? I hadn't given him much thought at all, apart from doing my best to avoid him when I was at school. Heat swamped me. Could I say if he hadn't been my Father confessor at school I wouldn't be sitting with him now, with his hand stroking mine?

I looked at him carefully, for the first time ever. His slightly greying hair had been brushed down flat with a most unflattering right parting. His eyes were a wintery gray, a colour I found chilling. His ears stuck out and his lips were large. I looked at the man opposite me and knew I would have to lie.

"You're very kind," I said shyly, thinking of the many penance prayers I'd had to say, after my confessions with him. Coffee arrived and I stopped, grateful for a momentary reprieve. I tried desperately, to think what else I could add. "And..."

"Do you see me as a man?" He interrupted. He spoke earnestly, leaning forward as the waitress moved away.

See him as a man? Of course, he was a man. He had to be a man. He was a priest for Heaven sake!

"Of course father," I replied feeling on safe ground. It was a no-brainer of a question. "Of course I see you as a man, you're a priest." I was puzzled. What had he expected me to say?

"Could you see me as a man and not a priest?"

Oh, Lord! This was getting worse. "In my eyes Father, you are first and foremost a man, always will be," I lied fearful he would see through me.

"Is that how you see me?" he murmured reaching once more for my hand which had inadvertently put down the teaspoon thereby making it available again.

He gently squeezed my fingers. "Thank you, Harmony." He smiled wistfully at me. "Call me Jerome."

"Yes, Father...eh Jerome," I returned resisting the overwhelming desire to look at my watch.

"It's very lonely being a priest," he said confidentially. "Sometimes I long for someone to confide in. I entered a seminary in Ireland when I was thirteen and since then my life has been one of deprivation and lack of companionship."

I sat still not daring to move lest I interrupted his thoughts and his need to share his deepest feelings with another human.

"Lately, I have longed to have someone close to me, someone, I could talk to."

I nodded. "I can understand."

"Do you?"

"Yes," I said softly. Truly, I understood. He had never had the warmth of a loving relationship. He had never experienced a mutual adult relationship given freely. Yes, he would be lonely. Was he looking for a way out of his present life? Was he hoping I would provide an escape route for him?

"I'm forty-five. Do you think I'm too old?"

Too old? For what?

The words almost burst from my lips but I managed to stem them. Here was a priest telling me how lonely he was. I was not about to tell him he was too old, for whatever it was he wanted.

"Of course not." I lied. It seemed every time I was around this priest, I felt compelled to lie. He was ancient from where I was stand-ing...sitting. Reverend Mother's advice about being suspicious of men above thirty was beginning to make sense. Among other things, they could be priests dressed up as ordinary men.

CHAPTER 32

"T his is Miss Brown," the Head Teacher, Mr Fernshaw said as we stood in front of forty pairs of eyes. "She will be your teacher for the year."

Silence fell and I was left alone to get to know my class. I opened the register and started to call out names, starting with Denis Avery and ending with Vanessa Yardley. Each child shouted, 'here,' as their names were called and I asked them to raise their hands so I could start committing names and faces to memory.

The morning was taken up dispensing exercise books, pencils and textbooks. Playtime came, and I was on playground duty. I stood in the playground watching children run screaming around chasing each other. A little girl came up and stood staring up at me without saying anything. She then reached for my hand and held it in hers, examined it minutely, turning it over and looked closely at my palm and the back of my hand.

"Your hands are brown," she said in wonder. "And your legs."

"Yes," I said. "They are."

"Are you brown all over?"

"Yes all over. Every bit of me is brown."

"Every bit?"

"Yes," I smiled down at her. What a strange question? How many children had never seen or been close to a *coloured* person?

She let go of my hand and ran off to a group of small children chanting, "She's brown all over. She's brown all over."

Lunchtime brought another surprise. Quite unexpectedly I was told I was to take over another class. The new teacher they'd had in the morning had refused to return after lunch saying her class were so badly behaved she would not stay.

My new class was filled with little seven-year-olds and I wondered how anyone could say they were unmanageable.

I entered the classroom and locked eyes with a little boy at the back of the class. I knew immediately he was, Darren Speed. I'd been warned about him as one of the most difficult children the school had ever experienced. At first glance, he looked innocuous sitting at the back of the class.

"If you have any trouble with him send him down to me," Mr Fernshaw had said as he led me to the classroom after the lunch break. "He spends most of his time outside my door, so don't feel bad about it."

I pushed open the classroom door and Darren and I clashed for the first time. In his hand, he held a conker (a chestnut tree seed), a large shiny brown conker attached to a piece of string. As the class looked at me with a mixture of curiosity and hostility, I heard Darren say, "Another one."

"Please put your conker away," I asked politely.

"No." he replied defiantly challenging me.

I decided to ignore him for the moment, but not to let it go.

"My name is Miss Brown," I said turning away from him, and picking up a piece of chalk wrote my name on the blackboard.

A little hand shot up and waved in front of me. A little girl in the front row, with brown hair caught up in a ponytail and large hazel eyes looked excited.

"Miss."

"Yes?" I acknowledged her raised hand.

"This morning our teacher was called Miss White. Are you called Miss Brown because you're brown?" I heard a snigger from the back,

Darren Speed. He looked at me and started banging his conker on the desk.

"No, my name is Brown because my father's name is Brown," I replied.

"My father is called Jim Cornell, and mine is different," a little voice called out.

"Mine is different too." Another voice cried.

"And mine," another voice said.

"Why are you brown?" another little voice interrupted.

"Where do you come from?" called another.

"If you want to ask me a question," I said loudly, "Put up your hand, then I will be able to answer all your questions in turn." I hoped I would gain some semblance of order as the class was quickly becoming noisy and I feared I'd soon have a riot on my hands.

The continual noise of Darren's conker hitting his desk added to the noise and I had a vision of the Mr Fernshaw rushing in to take control.

I picked up a small scissor from the pencil box on my desk and concealed it in my hand. I walked up and down between the rows of desks asking the children their names and what they liked doing most in school.

"My father says you people should go back to your own country," Darren said loudly from the back of the class.

I ignored him and continued my journey around the class until I reached his desk. "Darren," I said quietly. "Put your conker away. You can play with it at playtime."

He said nothing but continued smacking the conker against the top of his desk whilst staring at me defiantly.

"Darren, I will ask you once more." I did ask him once more and when he did nothing, I whipped the small scissor out and snipped the string, palmed the conker and walked quickly away.

A howl of unutterable rage went up behind me and I turned to see Darren throw his desk over and advance towards me. His face was contorted with fury, and I understood why the previous teacher had left in such a hurry. I stood my ground, Darren Speed, didn't know who he was dealing with. I was the girl Sister Agatha couldn't intimidate and I certainly wasn't going to let a seven-year frighten me.

"I'm going to tell, I'm going to tell," he screamed. "My dad will beat you up."

I moved and placed myself between him and the door.

"You can tell him anything you want," I told him calmly, "but you will have to wait until the end of school. And Darren, I would like to meet your father."

He stopped. A look of surprise crossed his face.

"Darren," I said softly, "You will get your conker back, but you didn't look after it too well, so now I will look after it until the end of school. Now go back to your desk."

He hesitated for a moment confused by my feigned calmness, and I took the opportunity to say to the other boys at the back of the room. "Help Darren with his desk so we can do some work before the bell goes."

I won't say it was the last spat Darren and I ever had during his year in my class, but we came to understand each other, and I was able to teach him to read. No other teacher seemed to have got close enough to him to be able to get any cooperation from him.

I never sent him out of my class for anything he did. I didn't believe in children wasting their time outside the Head teacher's door. I caught him once stalking me as I walked home. I felt I was being followed and turned around to catch a glimpse of him dodging behind a car. I casually led him down the road and in and out of numerous shops until I lost him or he gave up. He was one of the few children not met by a parent. I never told him I'd seen him following me.

Throughout the year Darren continued, at every opportunity, to insist reading was for stupid people. He said his father had told him so, and Darren idolised his father. I don't remember him ever mentioning his mother.

His father owned a chain of arcades with penny slot machines, and Darren told me he was very rich. He had five pounds a week pocket money and was very popular on the playground.

Darren was incredibly good at sums particularly addition and subtraction. I would often have him up to the blackboard to demonstrate his skill. I wanted to give him kudos for being good at something academic. I arranged the desks in my class into groups of six children and separated Darren from his cronies, placing him with a group of motivated able children. Though he always regarded me with suspicion, we maintained an uneasy truce and he shyly gave me a wonderful bunch of flowers at the end of the year.

CHAPTER 33

If the classroom was a possible war zone where vigilance was always required, the staffroom was open warfare.

"No, you can't sit there," I was told in a stage whisper during my first playtime break in the staffroom. "Miss Manley always sits there."

Miss Manley had been at the school longer than anyone could remember. Hardly surprising since the next longest serving teacher was Miss Everett and she'd only been there fifteen years. She sat quietly at the other end of the staffroom her face buried in the Times Educational Supplement as though she was hunting for another job.

"We do have some spare cups here for visitors," I was told. "We all bring our own mugs. I suggest you do."

Another member of staff, waiting to fill her mug from the urn said, "We all put money in the kitty at the end of each week to buy tea, coffee and biscuits."

I hadn't officially been introduced to the staff members but had seen them during morning assembly, so our first break-time together was a learning curve, a very steep learning curve.

"I would like to introduce you all to Harmony Brown," Mr Fernshaw said entering the staffroom to get a cup of tea.

"Hello, welcome," chorused the few voices of teachers standing around the large urn in the corner of the staff room.

"This is her first teaching post in London, so I hope you will all help her settle in."

"Come over here, young lady," a deep gruff voice called from the depth of the chair I had been warned to vacate. I looked across to a large woman, Miss Manley, Miss Emily Manley. She had dark eyes and pepper and salt hair, cut sharply at earlobe length.

"I'll leave you in the capable hands of Miss Manley," Mr Fernshaw said hurriedly and beat what looked to me like a hasty retreat.

I smiled and moved towards her. "Come and sit here next to me," she commanded and pointed to a vacant upright hard chair next to her comfortable armchair. "Miss Christie usually sits there, but she's on playground duty."

I sat balancing my cup and saucer with one hand and a tea biscuit in another.

"Now tell me, where you're from?"

The low chatter in the staffroom stopped, and I looked around to see all faces turn my way. It was becoming inappropriate to ask people where they came from as a means of introduction. There were many more *coloured* people in the big cities now and more arriving every day from the Asian subcontinent. Mr Enoch Powell had become a household name pushing the cause of white supremacy and fear of being over-run by nonwhites. His *'Rivers of Blood'* speech was famous and there were many people alarmed he may be right.

It had been a forgotten fact, that after the war, the West Indies were targeted with advertisements, as a place to recruit workers for the factories, transport systems and hospitals to help, in the regeneration of Great Britain. So first it had been the West Indians and then those from the Asian subcontinent coming to Britain looking for work, taking the jobs no one else wanted, hoping to make a better life for themselves and their families. They too had helped fight for their *Mother Country* in the war, and they too had lost many lives.

Miss Manley's direct question came as a surprise. She obviously couldn't place me.

I told her where my training college was, but she shook her head.

"No, no. I mean where do you *really* come from?"

I smiled. "Oh, I see," I said innocently. "I was born in Coventry."

She shook her head and gave a deep sigh as though dealing with a particularly cognitively challenged child. "I mean where do your parents come from?"

She was desperate to put me in a box, to classify me. She felt uncomfortable not knowing which box she could slot me into.

I smiled and stood up. "Goodness," I said sweetly. "That would take too long to tell you now... perhaps when we have more time."

"Smart," said a male voice behind me as I made for the door. "By the way, my name is Mario. Mr Caffarelli to the likes of Miss Manley. Take no notice of that old bag, she doesn't like WOGs either." With those words, he turned towards the playground as the bell rang out announcing the end of the break, though not before pinching my bottom.

Miss Manley and I arrived at the staffroom door at the same time and as I stood back to let her through she stopped, blocking my quick getaway.

"Watch yourself with that man," she said. "He's reprehensible when it comes to women. You know what Italians are like and he's got a wife and six children. It would help my dear if your skirts weren't so short."

She turned and strode determinedly towards the playground to collect her class. Her large wide rear encased and restricted in a thick brown tweed skirt pleated at the knee swung as she walked. She wore thick stockings with seams slightly askew running up the back of her legs and disappearing at her calf under the sensible length of her skirt. Her jacket matched her skirt, covering her wide hips and rounded stomach over a white blouse primly buttoned to her neck. Her shoes matched her outfit, brown sturdy brogues with pinwork in the leather.

As she walked by with her class, she smiled, "We'll find some time to be together," she whispered conspiratorially. It was at that moment

Darren Speed, first in the line of my class, looked at me, winked and chose to say. "What colour are your knickers today Miss."

The word, *knickers* sent all the children within hearing range into fits of giggles. I sent them up the stairs to the classroom ahead of me.

CHAPTER 34

I avoided the staffroom so as not to get drawn into the intrigues and petty arguments that made up the interactions between some members of staff. Miss Manley spearheaded the group that complained about Mr Fernshaw's management of children with behaviour problems, and Mario Caffarelli always took the opposite stance whatever the complaint.

Mr Fernshaw made a habit of dropping into my classroom at the end of the day, to ask how my day went and whether or not, I needed anything. At first, I thought it was out of concern for my being new to the school and having been given a tough class. But as time wore on, I realized it was an opportunity for him to vent his frustrations about the staff and the difficulties he was having with some of the parents.

"I've just had a visit from Father Keenan," he told me one day when he came into my class and stood by the window looking down onto the playground. "He said Mr Caffarelli was responsible for making his choir mistress pregnant, and she's had to go away."

"Oh dear," I murmured. I wasn't sure what I was supposed to say or indeed could say.

"I don't know what I can do about it," he continued. "He is a very good teacher, and the children and parents love him."

I wanted to say, it was really none of our business what two people, consenting adults, did after school.

"Of course he can't marry her, he's already married." Mr Fernshaw looked worried. "I don't know what I should do."

I was determined not to comment. Taking sides over staff issues knowing everybody had his or her allegiances was tantamount to professional suicide.

He gave a deep sigh. "And to make matters worse, he's always short of money and always borrowing from some member of the staff or other."

"But he does pay them back doesn't he?"

"Yes, eventually," Mr Fernshaw said. "He wouldn't get into debt if he didn't bet on the horses so much."

"Poor Mr Caffarelli," I murmured. "He must be worried having so many children."

Mr Fernshaw concurred. "Yes indeed. But now I'm really worried. He's taken the school sports cups to be professionally cleaned. He asked if he could, and I said yes. But Harmony," he dropped his voice, "I've heard, he's pawned them."

I nearly laughed aloud. "He's got time to get them back. It's not sports day for several months." I fought to keep a straight face. Mario certainly had ingenuity. Teachers were poorly paid, but with his six children, a wife, a future love-child and his gambling, he'd found ways to keep ahead of the game and still flirt.

"What would I say if Father Keenan asks where the sports cups are since the display cabinet is now empty?"

"That they're being cleaned?" I suggested.

"Yes of course." He fell into deep thought before leaving then said. "Good night, Harmony, see you tomorrow."

The saga of the sports cups came up again in June, just days before Sports Day. Mr Fernshaw dropped by my classroom during a lunch break and Mr Caffarelli and the sports cups came up again.

"I am getting worried," he said. "Mario still hasn't brought the cups back, and Sports Day is next week."

As the words came out of his mouth, Mario Caffarelli drew up in his car, opened the boot and lifted out several sparkling Sports cups and Trophies. Mr Fernshaw gave a deep sigh of relief and hurried out of my classroom.

Mario Caffarelli would also drop by and visit me in my classroom if I missed going down to the staffroom at break time. I went down to the staffroom intermittently as I didn't like the atmosphere of criticism and gossip. Truth be told, I also wanted to avoid Miss Manley.

"Just wanted to see how you're getting on," he said not long after Mr Fernshaw had told me about the choir mistress. "Don't believe everything you hear about me." He gave me a disarming smile.

"I hear very little about anybody."

"Good, because it's all lies."

I nodded and continued placing paint pots and drawing paper on each desk in readiness for the next lesson.

"By the way," he said as he reached the door. "Don't give the staffroom a complete miss, it will be taken by the queen bee, our Emily, that you're being unsociable. So show your face every now and again."

I opened my mouth to explain my wish to prepare for my lessons.

He stopped and held up a hand. "I know, I know, you're afraid Miss Manley will take a shine to you and make her girlfriend Bella Christie jealous."

I shuddered having witnessed one of Bella and Emily's fallings out at first hand.

Seeing a large middle-aged woman in brogues and tweeds stomp into the staffroom announcing, "I will never speak to Miss Christie again." Then break into floods of tears was not something I was in any hurry to repeat.

"How are things between them now," I asked side-stepping the inference I might make up a love triangle of some sort.

"Lovey-dovey," he said as he slipped out of my classroom.

CHAPTER 35

Not long after Mr Fernshaw had told me about Mario Caffarelli's expected love-child, things began to take on a different shape in the parish.

"It is a great worry for the church," Father Keenan said one Sunday from the pulpit, as we sat at Mass listening to one of his interminable sermons. "That more and more, I find myself marrying people of different religions. It is the duty of every single one of us who are not married to find a good Catholic husband or wife."

My mother shifted uncomfortably, she had married a non-Catholic and had spent twenty-five years of her married life praying for his conversion. My father was eventually worn down and converted.

"I have decided we will have a parish social, so our young people can meet each other."

The idea of a husband-finding social held no appeal, I had finished with men. I couldn't imagine putting myself out there, as though I was desperate. Besides, there were no *coloured* parishioners and being *coloured*, what chance did I have? And anyway, I was to be a nun.

We had recently moved from our rented flat in North London, to our own, albeit mortgaged, house, South of the river and our Parish,

St. Joseph's, was filled with white middle-class parishioners. I hadn't seen any remotely interesting men during any Sunday Mass. The majority of the parishioners were middle-aged and elderly women with a sprinkling of families with young children. Not much choice for any young women of the Parish looking for a good Catholic husband.

Father Keenan had decided a church social for the young people of the parish would be the best way forward. He set out on a recruitment drive by visiting families he knew or had heard of, with sons and daughters of marriageable age. He co-opted some of his faithful female middle-aged parishioners to help with the organization and *he* undertook the duties of the home visits.

Not long before Father Keenan's visit, my mother had a worrying experience. She'd received a strange and unsettling phone call. No, it wasn't a heavy breather, but rather, a gruff voice on the end of the phone.

"Is that a coloured house?" the voice asked.

Though shaken by the question, my mother was quick to reply. "The windows are green, and the front door is cream and green. So yes, it is a coloured house." She knew what the man on the end of the phone meant, as we were the only *coloured* family in the road. There had been some talk in the papers of house prices having dropped as a result of having *coloured* neighbours and house owners were getting angry.

The caller slammed the phone down at my mother's reply and she was frightened. "Quick Harmony," her voice harried as she pointed to the curtains. "Draw the curtains. No, don't put the light on. Draw the curtains first. We don't want any sniper outside taking pot shots at us, do we? Someone doesn't want us living here Harmony, otherwise, why would they phone and check if this was a *coloured* house?"

I gave a quick laugh hoping to pacify her. "Probably just a hoax, Mama,"

"No, I don't think so. With what's been going on in the newspapers and that politician, saying we ought to go home to our own country, we are not safe."

She was clearly upset. "This is my home. My father was English and I've been here since I was seven. Where would they send us back to?"

A bit difficult, I thought, since my father had been born in Cuba, had lived in Jamaica for fewer years than he'd lived in Cuba and had lived in Britain for decades. Where would he go if he were repatriated? Would he get a choice? Would he and my mother be split up? After all, she had been born in the Cameroons during the First World War when my Cornish grandfather, had taken West African troops to fight the Germans there. He had also taken his very pregnant African wife from the Gold Coast (now Ghana) to accompany him, and she had given birth in the temporary Army Hospital there. Repatriation could get very complicated...too complicated, I told my mother in an effort to reassure her as to the stupidity of the threat.

But her fears grew and from that day, as dusk fell, the curtains were drawn before the lights were switched on. We had to feel and stumble our way back across the room, bumping or falling over furniture, to the light switch.

The fear of being shot in our own sitting room by an unknown sniper prompted my mother to have extra bolts fitted. And anyone who came to the door had to identify themselves, by giving their full name, the nature of their business and if it was daylight, move to the bay window so that they could be assessed more fully before being granted admittance. Only when my mother, was satisfied, would she draw back the bolts, unlock the door, lift the latch and open the door. I would swear it would have been easier to get into Fort Knox then our house.

CHAPTER 36

One evening, as my mother was expounding her theory, yet again, on the reason behind the phone call, the doorbell rang and we both jumped.

"Don't open the door," she hissed reaching out to grab my arm.

"Don't be silly Mama," I said. "It might be someone we know."

"No one we know calls in the evenings."

I wanted to laugh but held back when I saw the fear on her face.

"Let me go," she said and pushed me aside.

She crept up to the door and stood to the side of the letterbox, in case, she confided to me later, a gun was pushed through.

She called out in a tremulous voice. "Who is it?"

"It's me, Mrs Brown," came a reply in a voice with an Irish accent we immediately recognised. "Father Keenan."

It was too dark to instruct him to stand by the bay window, so she withdrew the bolts, unlatched the door and let him in.

I'm not sure what he must have thought as he had listened to the bolts being drawn, the locks twisted and the door creak open slowly.

"Is everything alright?" His brow creased with concern as he stepped over the threshold.

"Of course, of course, why shouldn't it be? Come in." She held the door barely wide enough for him to slip in. It would hurt her pride to admit she was worried about anti-immigrant gangs hanging around outside ready to storm our house. She led the way into the sitting room.

"It's just that you sounded a bit..."

"We just like to make sure we lock up in the evenings," my mother hurriedly interrupted brushing aside his observations.

"Very good...very good. Better safe than sorry. You're not even safe in your own beds now," Father Keenan said reinforcing my mother's fears of there being evil lurking outside the walls of our home.

I saw her give a slight shudder. Such evil, she believed, was even more prevalent if you weren't white.

My mother, I knew, wouldn't mention the heightened danger of not being white to Father Keenan. She never wanted to draw anyone's attention to her colour.

"Would you like some tea Father?"

His eyes lit up and he smiled at her. "That I would, thank you kindly."

She looked at me, and I took it as my cue to put the kettle on. "Oh and, Harmony, I'm sure Father Keenan would like some of those crumpets."

"Thank you, yes." A look of joyous anticipation crossed his face.

Half listening to Father Keenan's voice from the sitting room, warning of the dire dangers surrounding us, I slipped the crumpets under the grill, smothered them in butter, tipped hot water over the tea leaves, placed the multi-coloured knitted tea-cosy over the teapot, and headed back to the front room.

Father Keenan was in the throes of his thesis on the wickedness of the world, firstly, being due to people not believing in the one true Catholic Church and secondly, to people not going to church very much anymore.

"Now what we need in this world to stop all this wickedness..." he reached for a buttered crumpet. "...is to get good Catholic youngsters together, marrying and producing offspring."

"Sugar, Father?" I proffered the sugar bowl, breaking into his lecture on the evils of the world, much of it gleaned from the popular press of which he was clearly an avid reader. During his interminably long sermons, he frequently referred to the horrors and scandals he'd read about to illustrate his point, that the devil was busy trolling the world, wrecking havoc and causing mischief.

My mother had her head dipped in the deferential stance she took in the presence of priests.

"As I always say, Mrs Brown..." He stopped mid-sentence, took three lumps of sugar and his eyes lit up at the sight of another toasted crumpet dripping with butter. "God Bless you, Harmony," he said as he reached for it. "You'll make someone a good wife."

I winced inwardly at the thought of marrying and living with someone as bigoted as Father Keenan, I gave him a small smile and excused myself pleading a headache.

"Oh, before you go, Harmony, it was you I came to see." He smiled. "I wanted to remind you about the church social on Saturday night.

I held my breath knowing what he was going to say next.

"I'm counting on you to be there to support the church."

"I'll make sure to be there Father." I lied having no intention of going anywhere near the place.

He nodded and turned back to continue his litany of the woes of the world. "The good Lord knows it's hard enough nowadays to reach out to young people with all that pagan music that's so popular. It's no wonder so many of them are falling off from Mass."

Was this Sister Agatha in a Priest's collar? It was no wonder the Church was losing ground. The words of popular songs had more relevance than any of Father Keenan's sermons.

CHAPTER 37

T he Church Social was deemed a great success and spoken of
with pride by Father Keenan, at Mass the following Sunday.

"The Saturday Social went down well," he said as he
stood proudly in the pulpit. "We were able to show that there are
many Catholics in our parish, young Catholics, youngsters who only
needed a chance to meet. And by the grace of God, good Catholic
marriages will be the outcome."

Of course, I went. In the end, it was easier to go than listen to my
mother reminding me every five minutes I would have told a big
unforgivable lie to Father Keenan if I didn't go. She was mortified she
may have to explain my absence, after Mass the next Sunday.

I arrived late and was met at the door by Father Keenan as he
returned from listening to confessions. He was still wearing his long
black cassock, his face aglow from the complements of all the middle-
aged women who'd chosen to go to his confessional rather than
Father Ignatius' confessional.

Father Ignatius was not a great orator. His sermons were incredibly simple and thankfully short. Though hailing from the Emerald
Isle, it was clear he'd never kissed the Blarney Stone. He tended to be
dour and didn't say his sermons in that soft seductive brogue so many

older women found irresistible in Father Keenan, our ageing Parish Priest.

Mind you, Father Ignatius didn't have time to woo his parishioners because he was into the nuts and bolts of running a church in a parish of fast receding churchgoers.

"If you don't put more money into the offering," he'd once said from the pulpit. "I'll have to turn off the heating during Mass."

He'd made a point of saying this during a sermon on the *generosity of spirit*, which turned out to be a diatribe on the lack of the *generosity of the pockets* of the parishioners. It had also been a particularly cold Sunday in January, making him even less popular. Consequently, the queue outside Father Ignatius' confessional became abysmally short. I always chose his, apart from being quicker, the penances he gave didn't incur too many prayers.

The good women of the parish were outraged at his threats to the heating and to show their disapproval they had taken to crowding into Father Keenan's confessionals and Mass.

"Good to see you, Harmony," Father Keenan said loudly above the latest pop song as I stepped through the door into the brightly lit church hall. "We have a license for a bar," he told me.

I slipped off my coat and handed it to a volunteer parishioner, took a raffle ticket for identification later and made my way into the hall.

I stood on the threshold and looked at the small group of young people jiggling to the latest record on the turntable.

"But only until eleven. So get going," Father Keenan added jovially behind me.

I smiled. "Thank you, Father."

I moved towards the row of empty seats lining the far wall, intending to fade into the background.

Before I could sit and take up my station as a wallflower, Barry rescued me.

"How about it?" he said appearing before me.

I nodded shyly, and he guided me onto the dance floor to watch him shake uninhibitedly as though he had uncontrollable twitches or was trying to adjust something in his trousers without the use of his hands. He was out of step with the pop song decrying the fact the Rolling Stones hadn't got any 'satisfaction', yet his face portrayed pure self-confidence as he moved and mouthed the words to the song.

That was how I had found Barry, or rather how he had found me. I learned he was a teacher at a local school and we talked as we danced together all evening. When he offered to take me home in his *vehicle*. I neglected to notice the word he used, *vehicle,* rather than a *car.* It shows you, how trusting I was.

His vehicle turned out to be an old Bedford van, which had seen better days, many better days and unaccountable miles. The sliding door fell off as he opened it with a flourish.

"My God!" I gasped stepping back.

"Just needs a little fixing," he said nonplussed and set about lifting the door back onto it slides. I stood back watching him curiously. He didn't seem at all put out by the incident, he appeared confident and so in control. I climbed into the passenger seat not sure if the van would make it home. It did, and that was the beginning.

Later I learned Barry wasn't a Catholic, even though I'd met him at a Catholic social in the overly brightly lit parish hall of St. Joseph's. He'd heard about the social, he told me, from some friends living nearby and had nothing better to do that evening. And much, much, later, he told me he'd come to the social, to meet a good Catholic girl. He'd needed a change as he'd recently broken up with his girlfriend.

"I'm a lapsed atheist," he'd said laughingly. I wasn't sure what a lapsed atheist was, so had joined in his laughter. He was different from any of the dates I'd ever had. He seemed to want to educate me. I found him a little condescending but forgave him because I thought he cared.

He took me to the Horniman's Museum to listen to a lecture on The Rare Bird's of Africa, on our first date. It was deadly dull, the hall was chilly and the chairs uncomfortable but it was free. He followed it by taking me to Olympia to watch Jimmy Hendrix on our second date. On our third date he took me to Ronnie Scott's Jazz Club, I thought him very sophisticated.

He then decided he would teach me to drive. He asked for thirty-five pounds to buy a car he had seen so I could practice. He didn't want me to drive his van. I was excited at the thought of owning a car and looked forward to a small easy to drive car, an old Ford or something similar, perhaps.

I was horrified when he drove up the next day in a large 1950s Chrysler car.

"A real bargain." he smiled proudly tapping the bonnet.

It was huge, with wings at the back extending the boot, a bench front seat and when I looked inside, saw the gear change was on the steering column.

"I can't drive this," I protested. "It's too big."

"It's perfect. It won't matter if you put a few dents in it. He opened the driver's door and encouraged me to sit behind the wheel. I slid behind the steering wheel and realised I couldn't see over the wheel, only through the wheel. Added to that, the bonnet stretched into infinity and I couldn't see the front end. I felt scared. "I can't..."

"Trust me, it will be all right," he interrupted. "This will be perfect."

So I did trust him and he took me to a nearby common where I was given my first driving lesson. It was when I drove over a few young sapling and surrounding bushes, he realised the Chrysler would not be perfect. I also realised I could not trust him completely, this was not the car to learn to drive in. We changed places, and he drove me home. I liked that he didn't get angry about the mistakes I made driving over young trees and bushes. He hadn't shout and was calm and encouraging during the disastrous first lesson. Perhaps, I thought, this was the man for me since my family had always said I could try the patience of a Saint.

When I told my mother about my driving lesson and Barry's patience she looked closely at me.

"You'll never get away from this one."

The tone of her voice indicated, she wasn't happy.

The only upside for my mother was, he was white, like her father. My father was not happy. But I was running out of options and I hadn't worked out which nationality, ethnic or religious group would be preferable as far as my family were concerned. I stuck to my plan to be a nun. That was until...

It didn't take long for Barry to seduce me and for me to discover that a life of celibacy was not for me. Hadn't Reverend Mother said I must go out and do things that young people did? I loved my introduction to sex.

My mother had once said that I must never have sex before marriage, as men did not marry such women. "You'll be considered second-hand goods."

I enjoyed the novelty of sex. But I knew I would have to marry him, so as not to be second-hand goods. Sex with Barry had reduced my options.

Barry, I reasoned, was kind, patient and experienced, had to be, he was thirty. I didn't ask him why he wasn't married. I knew I would accept anything he said. He gave the impression of being worldly and knowledgeable, and I liked that.

Most importantly, I felt reassured that he was not interested in me only for sex, I believed he loved *ME*... my mind and my personality.

He did, however, tell me years later, much later, I had been totally wrong. He was, essentially interested in me for sex, only sex, but had been careful not to give me that impression for fear I would reject him. Little did he know, my fear of being second-hand goods was greater than his fear of rejection.

"Where did you get the idea that men love women for their mind?" He'd grinned smugly after we were married and laughed at what he called my naivety and gullibility. This revelation was given after I'd had my children and lost the svelte figure of the woman he had married.

It had been impressed upon me that married women should stay married at all costs. Marriage was a sacrament and divorce was not only shameful but also, sinful.

"Once you've made your bed, you have to lie on it," my mother had once said. "Don't ever forget, the church excommunicates divorced people." I was stuck. I had to marry him and stay with him.

However, at the time I met Barry and being *awakened* by him, I believed it was the inner *ME* he was interested in, the inner *ME*, he liked and loved.

The memory of Mr O' Neil's abuse when I was ten, still dogged me. I carried a guilt I couldn't entirely eradicate. I still felt responsible for Mr O' Neil putting his hands up my skirt and inside my knickers.

Barry helped to lessen the guilt that sex was in some way dirty, though the belief it wasn't *nice,* remained buried deep within my psyche. I liked sex with Barry. I hoped he didn't see me purely as a sex object. At the beginning of our relationship, Barry made me believe he loved me for being a good person, a nice person, not only because he thought, I was sexy.

CHAPTER 38

Barry took me to meet his family, a bold move on his part I thought, and a highly significant one for me. Obviously, he wasn't ashamed of me and didn't care what his family thought of my being *coloured*. Ergo, it must mean he wasn't only interested in me as a *coloured* girl to add as a notch to his belt of exotic experiences.

His Aunt Ada and Uncle Stan were the first of the family I was to meet. It wasn't until we stood on the doorstep of their little pebble dashed council house in Croydon, I realised there was a possibility they were not prepared.

"Have you told them?" I asked nervously as Barry rang the bell.

"Told them what?" he returned, a devilish smile on his face.

My heart sank with dismay. I recalled the time I had been taken home to meet Peter's parents and the patent dislike I'd experienced at the hands of his mother. Was I about to be subjected to such rudeness again? Fear of impending humiliation engulfed me. Was I once more, to be faced with rejection based purely on the colour of my skin?

Barry looked at me. "What do I have to explain?" He gave a careless shrug. "I simply said I was bringing a friend to tea, and my aunt was happy."

Before I could reply the door opened and the smile on Aunt Ada's face solidified as her eyes swept over me for the first time.

There was a fraction of a second when the door shook in response to her tightened grip on the handle and I thought she might slam the door in my face.

I smiled tentatively. "Hello."

Wiping her hands on her apron, she stepped back allowing us to enter. "Come in. Come in dearie. You're not quite...." She hesitated before finishing her sentence as her eyes swung accusingly to Barry. "Er...Barry said he was bringing a friend."

Barry stopped her by giving her a hug followed by a laugh, clearing enjoying her reaction.

Nervousness gripped my heart as I stepped over the threshold. The idea of spending time with people who actively disliked me for no other reason than I wasn't the right colour, caused bile to rise in my throat. I swallowed hard and forced myself to smile shyly as I watched Aunt Ada fondly greet her nephew.

"Oh Barry, you naughty boy, what will your mother say?" she whispered as he bent to kiss her wizened cheek. She turned back to me. "Come into the parlour dearie, it's cold out there."

I was ushered into the front room and introduced to Uncle Stan, a thickset man with bushy eyebrows, and a wide mouth devoid of teeth in both his upper and lower jaws. His brows drew together as he saw me and then he quickly displayed his gums in a smile.

"This is Harmony, Stan. Barry's new friend." Aunt Ada said loudly. "You sit here dearie."

She led me to a chair near the hearth and close to her husband. The chair was placed so I could get the full blast of heat from the coals burning in the small grate. "Move your chair closer to the fire. You must be cold luv."

She turned and quickly made her way to the door.

"Come on Barry, you can help me bring in the trifle."

A white lace tablecloth covered the surface of the table, on which stood a large cut-glass bowl of pink blancmange, a bowl of red jelly, a plate of jam sandwiches, a plate of bread and butter, a small dish of tinned pink salmon and a Victoria sponge seeping strawberry jam and dusted with icing sugar.

I was left with Uncle Stan, a roaring coal fire and a table already heavy with the makings of a very British high tea.

My eyes slid around the small front parlour crammed with large round edged furniture of nineteen thirties vintage.

A large sideboard topped with bric-a-brac from holidays spent in Margate and Broadstairs stood against one wall over which hung a plaster relief of flying geese with, *Holiday in Margate* painted in bright colours beneath the tail feathers.

"Ello luv," Uncle Stan said as my eyes returned to him. He observed me from under thick bushy eyebrows, his expression both curious and wary as his eyes watched my every move. His toothless gums caused his upper lip to pleat as his lips came together and he considered what to say next.

Belatedly he pulled his shirt across his chest, fastening the buttons to cover his string vest as though he'd suddenly realised he was partially undressed and gave a little cough before engaging me in conversation.

He spoke slowly and loudly enunciating every word carefully as though I was not only hard of hearing but lacked the wherewithal to understand him.

"I work with darkies," he declared as a way of opening up a conversation. He nodded his head sagely and looked at me kindly in an effort to put both of us at ease.

I looked at him not sure if he was teasing me or how I should respond. But Uncle Stan was serious. His face creased as he earnestly leaned towards me. I knew he wanted to reassure me he meant me no harm and didn't mind I was a *coloured* person sitting in his parlour on a Sunday afternoon.

"Oh," I responded devoid of any ideas of how to react.

"It would be all right if they were all like you luv," he offered by way of making sure I hadn't taken offence.

I gave a half-smile, again not sure how to respond.

"But them darkies I work with are always complaining. They're always saying they want to go home. Why did they come here then?" He hesitated and paused, before adding, "But it's alright because I can see you're different."

I nodded as words tumbled around in my head, useless words, meaningless words and platitudes to put him at ease. But in the end, I remained silent. Uncle Stan's attempt to engage me in conversation was excruciatingly embarrassing for both of us. The more he talked the bigger his feet got until all his prejudices were laid bare.

"Them darkies should go back to their own country since they don't like it here. We don't want them anyway. They come over here taking our jobs and...." He stopped as Barry came into the room a broad grin on his face.

"Aunt Ada makes the most delicious trifles."

And with a dramatic flourish placed the large cut-glass bowl on the table. "She always puts a lot of sherry in it."

"Looks good."

I was relieved he'd arrived. I smiled at him, hopeful he would stay and Uncle Stan would stop talking about darkies.

"Glad to see you two have hit it off." Barry grinned at us, turned and left the room. I was once more alone with Uncle Stan as he struggled to find something to say.

Uncle Stan's sentiments were not new, I'd heard them many times before. I didn't feel angry hearing them again. I longed to find the words to reassure him, put him at ease, but what could I say?

"Don't take it badly luv," Uncle Stan said as Barry left the room. "I'm not talking about you. I don't mind 'em coming to our country if they fit in, like you."

I touched my straightened hair. He'd hit the nail on the head. I was trying to fit into his world, straightening my hair was evidence enough. He smiled at me.

Somehow the thought, I was so eager to *fit in,* didn't make me feel good.

"Yes, I see," I murmured in a conciliatory tone. "What work do you do?"

"I used to paint houses but I'm afraid I'm laid off you see, luv. It's me back you see. I can't work. The doctor has laid me off. "

How could Barry have done this to me? I asked myself half listening to Uncle Stan telling me about his bad back. Not only did I find the whole situation unbearable, it was also evident Uncle Stan was feeling the same way. He kept coughing and shuffling his slippered feet as though he longed to get up and go anywhere but here. I sympathised with him. We each shared the same longing.

Stan and Ada should have been prepared, given the choice as to whether or not they wanted a *darkie* in their home, sitting in their front room, on a Sunday afternoon.

Inside I was a seething cauldron of anger and frustration, not at Stan, but at Barry for putting me in such a position and had I responded in the way I wanted...the course of my life would have been very different.

CHAPTER 39

As I sat in Aunt Ada and Uncle Stan's house, feeling angry with Barry, I knew I would have to marry him, come what may. I acknowledged, I was now *second-hand goods*. My choices were abysmally limited. I had blown any possibility of becoming a nun as I'd planned, having broken the vow of chastity. Barry was my only hope. Had things been different... I had to stop thinking like that... there was no point.

I'd been taught to be polite whatever the situation and sitting in Aunt Ada and Uncle Stan's front room was a test of my upbringing. I would have loved to walk out, politely of course, loved to get away from people who were condescending on the strength of the colour of their skin. Was I being too sensitive? I don't think so.

However, I did nothing. Instead, I sat primly, a smile stuck to my face, wishing I was anywhere but in the small cramped front room, with people who considered their superiority so great, based purely on being white, they could say virtually anything to people they considered inferior. Aunt Ada and Uncle Stan were totally oblivious to their prejudices. They didn't mean to be rude.

Uncle Stan rose to place more coal on the fire, piling it on until the room was filled with smoke. We both coughed, and my eyes watered with the smoke.

"I expect you're cold luv," he said kindly as he turned to look at me over his shoulder.

I shook my head. "No. I'm fine, thanks," I spluttered.

"I'll get some more coal for the fire." He picked up the coal bucket and made for the door.

"Put your teeth in Stan," Aunt Ada called from the kitchen. "Your tea's nearly ready."

I could hear her talking to Barry and the tone of her voice told me she was admonishing him. I knew it was about me. I stood and moved closer to the door.

"I won't tell your mother," she said in a stage whisper. "You'll have to tell her yourself."

Barry laughed. "About what?"

"About 'er, your *coloured* girlfriend."

Barry laughed. "What difference is it going to make to her?"

"Oh, you are a one, Barry." Aunt Ada laughed back at him. "I'll let you tell her."

I leapt away from the door as Uncle Stan, his hand's full with the overflowing bucket of coal and a shovel, shouldered his way into the room.

"You alright luv?"

I nodded hiding my disappointment at missing the rest of the conversation between Barry and his Aunt.

More coal was heaped on the fire, despite it being already full, and thick smoke converged up the chimney. Uncle Stan sat down, pleased with his efforts. "That should do."

"Stan," Aunt Ada called.

Uncle Stan ignored her, his eyes fixed on me. "Do you know Desmond Collingwood?" he enquired leaning back in his seat. "I used to work with him. He comes from the same place as you."

I shook my head trying desperately to fathom why I should know Desmond Collingwood.

"Where does he come from?" I found myself asking for the sake of something to say.

"He comes from the same place as you. Jamaica. Quite a lot of the darkies I work with come from there."

I hadn't told him where I came from, yet he'd assumed both Desmond Collingwood and I were countrymen.

"I'm afraid I don't know your friend." I did what we British do so well, readily admit to being afraid.

You know, we say... "*I'm afraid I can't...I'm afraid it's not possible...I'm afraid I can't come...I'm afraid I don't know.*" Yes, we are always afraid...basically, we're afraid of straight talking.

"No. He's not my friend luv," Uncle Stan interjected quickly. "Thought you might know him, being that you come from the same place and you look the same." He looked disappointed. I schooled my expression to neutral.

We were interrupted by Aunty Ada's appearance carrying a large teapot swathed in a brown knitted tea-cosy.

"Stan put your teeth in, you can't eat without them," she told him impatiently.

Uncle Stan rose and shambled off towards the kitchen.

"Sorry about that dearie," she said turning to me. "He would have put them in if he'd known it was you coming."

She rearranged the place settings and beckoned me to the table. "You best sit by the fire dearie. You must find it very cold in this country."

I looked at Barry closely following behind his aunt and met his eyes, appealing for his intervention, but instead got a grin of approval.

"Yes," Uncle Stan concurred returning, his mouth shaped in a natural setting around large teeth that slipped for a moment, quickly replaced by large hands. "It's hot in your country."

"Actually, I was born in Coventry," I said taking my seat. I hoped this knowledge would reassure both Aunt Ada and Uncle Stan I wasn't feeling cold and despite looking different, I was, in fact one of them...born and brought up in England.

"Really dear?" Aunt Ada said abstractly as she moved a plate of bread already buttered and pushed a small dish of tinned pink salmon towards me. "Help yourself to some salmon, dearie."

"Coventry you say," Uncle Stan said large teeth biting into a jam sandwich. "So, in Africa, they call some of them towns the same as ours."

His observation left me stunned. I picked up a triangle of bread and butter to cover my desire to laugh and helped myself to a morsel of tinned salmon.

"Must be one of the smaller towns," Stan continued knowingly. He reached for a slice of the Victoria Sponge, but his hand was slapped away by Aunt Ada.

"Eat some more bread and butter," she ordered. "You need to fill up the corners before you start on the cake."

Uncle Stan's response was unintelligible as he picked up a slice of bread and butter. He didn't look happy and glared at his wife.

"Turn on another bar of the eclectic fire, Stan," Aunt Ada requested ignoring her husband's angry glare. "Harmony isn't used to the cold. Are you dearie?" She turned to me for confirmation.

"I'm fine," I gasped as Uncle Stan moved the electric bar heater next to me and switched on another bar. Between mouthfuls of salmon, bread and butter, bread and jam, blancmange, jelly and finally the Victoria sponge cake, having refused the trifle, I sat slowly baking, sweat running in cold rivulets between my shoulder blades.

The coal fire in the grate burned fiercely. A two-barred electric fire was placed so that its radiant heat beamed directly onto me, to ensure I received all of its heat. The room was turned into a furnace. Surely they too must find the heat unbearable? But they gave no sign, not even Barry.

Throughout my visit, Uncle Stan never stopped talking about how hot it was in my country. Aunty Ada obsessed with ensuring I was warm enough, constantly asked if I were cold. I could have been speaking a foreign language since she didn't appear to hear my replies telling her I wasn't in the least bit cold.

Being a painter decorator, Uncle Stan was at great pains to explain how he had hurt his back and therefore was unable to work. "I fell off a ladder, you see, Luv. Them darkies are much better at climbing. I suppose they're used to climbing up all them coconut trees back there, in their country."

Out of the corner of my eye, I saw Barry grinning. I shot him a silent pleading look begging him to save me from any more of Uncle Stan's observation of his *darkie* workmates. I got the distinct impression Barry was enjoying laughing at everyone, including me. A cruel streak possibly, one I should have noted ...but missed.

I sat on the edge of my seat as Uncle Stan continued to share his knowledge of Africa and Jamaica.

"Jamaica must be a very big town in Africa," he observed in between Aunt Ada fussing with the large teapot and her Victoria sponge. "They all seem to come from there... them darkies...where I work." He smiled at me. I held my breath as he clicked his rather large teeth back into place and sucked deeply anchoring them firmly onto his gums.

I toyed momentarily with the thought of giving a brief geography lesson, but gave up, admitting defeat. Aunt Ada and Uncle Stan were happy with their knowledge of the world.

Though they had subjected me to their limited world knowledge and the agony of the equatorial heat of their front parlour, they were both kind and caring. Despite my being the first *coloured* person they'd hosted in their home, they had done their best to make me feel welcome.

CHAPTER 40

Tea with Aunt Ada and Uncle Stan was a prelude to my initiation to Barry's family. I was soon to meet his parents.

Not wanting to appear distrustful of the man I had already slept with...alright, we hadn't done much sleeping... had sex with, I neglected to question him in detail as we drove up North to spend New Year with his parents, if they knew I wasn't white.

Barry told my parents he wanted to take me to meet his family and teased them by saying he would take me in exchange for his television. I hasten to add, we didn't own a television as my parents were vehemently against having one, despite my father being in show business and had even been on television. Being fixated on a small screen, they'd said, interfered with family conversations.

As we drove up North, Barry glanced at me smiling. "My parents are looking forward to meeting you." He placed his hand proprietarily on my thigh whilst negotiating a particularly difficult manoeuver around a large lorry. I gasped, fearful if he didn't concentrate, we wouldn't make it around the lorry.

There you are then, I told myself, all was well with his parents. They were expecting me, even looking forward to meeting me. I felt comforted, nothing to worry about, Mr and Mrs Purvis, had been told I was *coloured*.

But then, as we stood on the doorstep, I had an overwhelming premonition Barry had, committed a lie of omission. Had Barry omitted to tell his parents the whole truth about me? Did it really matter? Would his parents be in for a shock? I checked.

"You did tell them, didn't you?" I asked with visions of being refused entry to Barry's parents' home.

Having experienced years of rejection based purely on the colour of my skin, being refused a flat, being refused holiday jobs as a student, being refused so many things, I couldn't take another rejection.

What would I do? I now couldn't be a nun, as I'd already broken the vow of chastity. My options had run out. Barry was my only hope.

My anxiety at having to face the condescending treatment I'd experienced so often from people who thought they were superior and demonstrated this by treating me as though I was another species, escalated.

What was I going to face? Another uncomfortable meeting as I'd experienced with Barry's Aunt and Uncle who'd had no idea their treatment did little to make me feel accepted or comfortable?

"Why worry?" Barry looked at me a small smile playing on his lips. "What's there to tell?" His reply confirmed I was right. It was the reply, I dreaded.

"I'm not white. How will they take it?"

"My parents won't care."

"Barry, they might..." I started and then stopped as the door swung open.

A small brown-haired woman stood in the doorway, and my heart fluttered nervously. A smile froze on her face as her eyes fell on me, her mouth dropped open at the beginning of the greeting she was about to make.

A moment of silence followed, I smiled nervously aware of Barry stepping forward to sweep his mother into his arms.

"Hello mum," he said. "Aren't you going to invite us in?"

"Oh, Barry you are a one. You're always full of surprises. Come in my dear," she said as she stepped back from her son and opened her arms expansively towards me. "Dad and I have been looking forward to meeting you."

I stepped over the threshold and into my new life, unaware at the time, these people would one day be my family.

I didn't get a chance to talk to Barry, I wanted to tell him what I felt about his omission in telling his parents about me, but he was shepherded hurriedly into the kitchen under the pretext of helping with coffee and biscuits. I was left, after a brief introduction, with his father, Earnest Purvis.

I was pleasantly surprised. Earnest made no mention of my being foreign, a darkie, coloured or different. He didn't even ask me where I came from. We talked about the weather, the roads, and the journey up the M1 and what I did for a living.

Saying I was a teacher had an immediate positive effect and by the time Barry and his mother returned with a tray of coffee and biscuits, I was being quizzed about my views on the modern education system as opposed to how it had been in Earnest's day.

"Things have gone downhill, since my day," he informed me. "We were not allowed to answer our teachers back."

"Yes dear," Dora Purvis said as she entered the room catching the tail end of our conversation. "Things have got worse." She placed a cup of extraordinarily milky coffee on the small table beside me. "If there's not enough milk in yours, tell me dear and I'll heat up some more."

Coffee with hot milk! I blanched. Hot milk! I sipped my coffee gingerly and slowly, whilst listening to Barry telling his parents about his work. His mother beamed with pride.

"My Barry is very clever you know. He was always top of his class in primary school. He passed his eleven plus to go to the grammar school." She smiled fondly at her son. This was not the right time to mention my disastrous failure with the eleven plus. I watched her as she looked proudly at her son.

"Waste of time," his father mumbled. "Didn't do him much good. He failed all his O'Level exams."

Barry opened his mouth as he turned to his father but Dora Purvis sensing trouble quickly intervened. I got the feeling she was used to being the peacemaker between father and son.

"Don't be so hard on him Earnest. He's done well now, haven't you son?"

I looked at Barry and he winked at me. "Harmony knows I'm clever, don't you?"

Both his parents turned to look at me expectantly. I took a sip of coffee and gave what I hoped, would appear to be a nod. Why were they so hung up on Barry being clever?

"Of course you are." Dora Purvis beamed at her son. "He went to grammar school."

Earnest gave a grunt, dunked a biscuit in his cup and took a bite out of the soggy mess before settling back in his chair and stretching his legs towards the coal fire.

"Barry has been telling me all about you." Dora turned back to me not before throwing her husband an anxious look. She was clearly determined to turn the conversation back to safer ground...me.

I looked at Barry. What in heaven's name had he been saying about me?

"He's a naughty boy for not telling me about you before you came. And I'm going to have words with Ada too. She's my sister and I would have thought she would have warned me. I only spoke to her the other day, and she said you'd been to tea, but she told me nothing about..." she stopped, looked away and quickly started to gather up the coffee cups. "I better get these washed," she mumbled.

Earnest Purvis gave a little cough. "Harmony has been telling me about her job." He looked slightly pink as though embarrassed about his wife referring to me as being something she should have been warned about. "She teaches little children."

"Oh yes," Dora Purvis said. "Barry told me. You speak ever such good English dear, better than me."

Was I expected to answer her observation about my English language skills? Should I thank her for the compliment? I suspected, my speaking *good* English, in her mind, made up for my not being white. I curved my lips into a small smile and quickly offered to help take the cups into the kitchen.

"Thank you, dear," Dora said and led the way.

She closed the door quickly behind us and stood against it. "Now dear," she said in a stage whisper. "You mustn't mind Earnest. It was all a bit of a surprise...you know what I mean." She paused and turned to replace the remaining biscuits in a tin. "Not that we mind," she added hurriedly and moved to the sink quickly filling it with hot water and a drop of washing- up liquid. "I'll wash if you don't mind, and you can dry."

I picked up the tea towel and moved to the draining board. We were silent, as we stood side-by-side working as a team, one washing, the other drying and stacking.

"How well do you know Barry?" she asked suddenly.

"Well, we only met..."

"My Barry is very creative," she interrupted and continued hurriedly. "That's why he's so moody. Thought I ought to warn you. His father doesn't understand him."

Of course, I didn't realize it then, but his moodiness, long periods of silence and sarcastic cutting remarks were going to be the order of the day and would be insidiously destructive in our relationship and to my self-esteem.

"Barry has always been a bit of a rebel. He's always liked to shock us. It's the reason why he and his Dad don't get on. He used to like to dress up when he was young and his father was worried he might be... " She hesitated and quickly changed the subject. "But he and I are very close. I wasn't one bit surprised to see you, dear. I always knew Barry would bring someone different home one day, only I thought he'd bring home a Chinese girl, he likes them."

Barry came into the kitchen and interrupted us. "What are you two girls gossiping about?" he said teasingly.

"Oh, Barry you are a one." It appeared to be her favourite phrase. She laughed adoringly up at her son, her blue eyes twinkling proudly.

I spent the week with them, everyone working hard to avoid mentioning the, *coloured elephant*, in the corner of the room...ME.

Although when we were alone, Dora did bring it up again.

"I'm not happy Ada didn't tell me. It was a shock you know dear, and I'll be having words with her about it." She sniffed and then smiled at me. "I hope you didn't notice how my mouth fell open when I opened the door and saw you."

I assured her I hadn't noticed. I felt sorry Aunt Ada hadn't told her about me. I hoped it didn't cause a rift between them.

"Nobody would be prejudiced if they were all like you, my dear," she said.

I shuddered.

The morning before I left, Earnest Purvis found me alone in the sitting room and sat down opposite looking worriedly at me.

"Just want to check how well you know Barry?" He asked hurriedly in a low voice.

"We met two months ago," I replied. His furtive manner puzzled me.

"You seem such a nice young, innocent girl," he said and gave a little cough. "Barry is well..." His words hung in the air, soft eyes searching my face. "Barry is...well... not..."

Dora came bustling in to announce breakfast was ready, stopped and looked suspiciously from her husband to me her brows creasing.

"What are you two whispering about?" she asked sharply. "Come on both of you, breakfast is ready. The tea will get cold."

I never got to hear what Earnest Purvis wanted to tell me about Barry.

As our visit came to an end, Dora Purvis told me about Barry's past girlfriends all of whom she'd felt weren't good enough for her son. I listened, wondering what she really thought of me? Was I good enough? I doubted it, I was coloured. Dora Purvis frequently reassured me that my English was very good, *better than her English,* and added, I sounded very posh, this thereby, allowed her forgive my colour.

I was aware she and Barry were frequently huddled in the kitchen talking in lowered tones. They would stop if I entered and quickly change the subject. Of course, I asked Barry about it.

"It's your imagination, why would we be talking about you?"

I tried to believe him, wanted to believe him, and so ignored my intuition that he hadn't told me a lie of omission, but a blatant lie. It's easy to deny the obvious when it doesn't suit what we want. But the niggling feeing I'd been lied to remained.

On returning home, my own parents had ordered their own television. Barry always said it was like taking whisky to the *Red Indians*. It only took a week and already they were addicted to the small screen.

CHAPTER 41

Barry proposed as we were driving across the Atlas Mountains in Morocco. We were in his beloved vehicle, the Bedford van. Its door still fell off if it was pulled back with any hint of force, and he would mumble, "*oaf,*" if anyone but he, pulled it off.

I thought the setting of his proposal very romantic. We were travelling with four of his friends, two other couples, and it was swelteringly hot inside the van. Ragged outcrops of hills stretched before and around us, and the sun shimmered off the tarmac strip ahead giving a mirage of water in the distance.

Barry hated to stop once he got behind the wheel and any suggestion that we would like to admire the view or take photographs was met with derision.

"Buy a postcard," he'd say and put his foot down.

We were in a remote spot when we were first forced to stop. A row of rocks had been placed across the road. As the van slowed, men jumped out from behind rocks at the side of the road and advanced towards us.

The leader shouted at us in broken English. "We have hashish. You buy?"

We shook our heads.

"No," Barry called back and with a flick his hand shouted... "imshi, imshi."

He was very proud of the little bit of Arabic he had picked up whilst doing National Service in Libya.

"Cheap," the dark-eyed man said stepping closer. "Very good quality."

"Imshi," Barry reiterated and pointed to the rocks blocking the road.

The man shrugged, stepped back and gestured to his companions to clear the road. As we drove off, they made signs with their hands that could be interpreted as not very flattering.

It was after that incident, Barry proposed and I said yes. I didn't dare risk being second-hand goods and left on the shelf, so I accepted his proposal.

I imagined a traditional engagement ring when we returned from our holiday. But Barry had other ideas. "I don't believe in engagement rings," he said. "A waste of money."

God knows why, but I accepted his view of the value of an engagement ring and so never got one, ever.

But we did celebrate our engagement. Barry stopped in a small village in the Atlas Mountains. He saw a small stone house with a sign outside. It was a small restaurant, someone's house, with its tiny room set out with stools and small metal tables. We were proudly led to a wood fire in one corner, on which sat a huge pot. The menu was limited, and as the restaurateur, a grubby looking man with dirty hands lifted the lid, I forced myself not to retch.

"Good. Yes?" He picked up a large spoon and stirred a greasy stew with unrecognizable shapes of meat floating deep within. Was that a fly?

"Looks good," Barry said virtually smacking his lips and ordered six portions. "This is on us." He told the others. A look of consternation swept across their faces before they thanked him. "To celebrate our engagement."

I declined my bowl of...not sure what, by pleading a lack of appetite and more a need for fluids.

"Good, cheap and satisfying," Barry said as we returned to the van. "Shame you weren't hungry Harmony."

For the rest of the day, Barry needed urgent comfort breaks. He'd slam on the breaks, screech to a stop and leap from the van. Memories of him running towards sparse outcrops of rocks have remained with me.

CHAPTER 42

O n returning from Morocco, we told his parents we
planned to marry.

"I always wished I'd had the nerve to do the things
Barry did," Dora said when we were alone. "He is so unconventional."
She accepted me because I was her son's choice and since she thought
that everything he did was outrageously wonderful, she would not
reject his future bride. "But what about the children?" She later asked.
"They will be half-caste." She sounded worried.

"So what," Barry returned sharply. "Harmony and I are the same
species."

My own parents were less pleased. There was a heartbeat of
silence when I announced my intention to marry Barry. My mother
looked away, and my father's expression showed disapproval. They
voiced no opposition as they could see I was determined to
marry him.

Despite being a teacher, I still had to be home by midnight and
contend with intrusiveness into every aspect of my life. Should Barry
be visiting, on the dot of midnight my mother would appear and tell
him to leave, as it was she said, "another day." She explained that he

had only dated me for a day and midnight was the beginning of another day and they wanted to go to bed.

In retrospect, I was determined to get away from the control and strictness of home life and not be cast in the role of second-hand goods.

My mother warned me against having a long engagement. "Six months is the optimum time for an engagement." She looked at me meaningfully. What did she mean? She sighed and added. "The Royal family, never have long engagements."

I tried not to laugh, but just then the phone rang and she turned to pick up the receiver. Later I asked her why she'd said my engagement was to be no more than six months.

"What difference would it make if we don't get married for a couple of years?" I was puzzled. I would have liked a longer engagement, but then I didn't have the strength to go against my mother's wishes. I wasn't sure how she would react.

"It's a long time to wait." She turned away indicating that her response should be good enough and no further questions were needed.

"For what?" I persisted.

"Your awakening," she returned. "Why do I have to be so explicit?"

Awakening?

"Once you've had your awakening you won't be able to leave it alone." She said, turned and walked out of the room making it clear she'd finished her discussion of sex.

I'd already had my awakening, my concession to the free love ideals of the sixties, and it wasn't something I would find hard to leave alone. In the beginning, I'd thought it wonderful, but there were times I now found it utterly boring. So boring in fact, Barry had once caught me unwrapping a boiled sweet I'd spied on his bedside table. He hadn't been happy, as he'd been working so hard to reach a climax. I'd apologized of course and had tried to concentrate on the job at hand. Now I was being told, once I'd experienced my awakening I wouldn't be able to leave sex alone!

I laughed at her retreating back.

"It's not anything to laugh about," she snapped when she found I had followed her into the kitchen. "Also, you don't want to get married less than three months after you announce your engagement because people will think that you had to get married."

I sighed and planned my wedding date, no longer than six months and not less than three months after our engagement was announced.

My future Mother-in-law was more pragmatic. She was mainly concerned about what colour outfit my mother would be wearing so their colour schemes wouldn't clash.

Over a quiet cup of tea, Dora became relaxed and chatty. "Mrs Williams, from next door, was asking me just the other day, what I felt about having a *coloured* daughter-in-law," she said. "People are curious you see dear."

"Oh," I murmured, not quite sure how I was supposed to react.

"Well," Dora continued with a tone of contrived pride as though she was about to give me a great compliment, one I should be grateful to receive. "I said, you speak *ever such good English,* better than me, and having a *coloured* daughter-in-law in the family is..."

"Black," I interjected stopping her.

She stilled looking puzzled. "Black?"

I felt suddenly free, liberated. I didn't care what she thought. The civil rights movement in America had grown a pace and Black people now made no concession to anyone, no apology for their colour. We were black, not *coloured*. Yes, black, and black is beautiful. Every bit of being black is beautiful. Our colour in all its shades is beautiful. Our hair, yes, our hair is beautiful too. Black people no longer had any need to straighten their hair to be like everyone else. Hair, natural hair is beautiful.

I was black and it was wonderful being able to say it and say it with pride. I was even considering giving up straightening my hair and going Afro. Though I hadn't dared yet, in deference to my future in-laws. They may need to get used to one change at a time, first, my being black, and then eventually, my hair in its natural state.

"Black...I'm black," I repeated proudly.

"Black?" Dora's eyes opened wide in shock. "Oh no dear," she gasped horrified at such a concept. She bent forward, reached for my hand and patted me compassionately. "Not black dear. Of course you're not black. Whoever gave you that idea? You're not *reeeelly* black, You're a nice...um...honey colour ...dear. Don't call yourself black. No dear, No. It's not nice."

She followed her words of sympathy by making sure I understood she forgave my blackness. "Besides dear, you speak better English than me. I always tell my friends your English is posh."

I looked at her with pity. This was a woman who would be a grandmother to my children, her son's children. How was she going to cope with being grandmother to black children? What colour would they be to her? I doubt she would call them black. But I would.

I would make it my mission, to bring my children up proud of their blackness, however much black my children had running through their veins. I would make sure they would be proud, very proud of being black.

CHAPTER 43

I n keeping with my mother's wishes, my marriage took place six months later, not too long to wait for my awakening, and not too soon for it to be, a shotgun wedding.

I was married in the small chapel at the Convent school where I'd been a pupil and where I had asked Reverend Mother if I could join them as a nun. Sister Rose, my old piano teacher, played the organ.

Friends and family came from far and wide and the nuns, who'd taught me at school, filled the choir stall.

As I stood at the entrance to the chapel, on the cusp of becoming a wife, my hand on my father's arm, my prayer book and flowers in my hand, my mother kissed me on my cheek and held me close for a moment. She stepped away, still holding me and looked deep into my eyes giving me a sad smile.

"I should have told you before now." Her eyes flicked to my father in warning.

A sense of doom washed over me as I stood in my wedding finery. I set my lips tight and waited, worried at what she was about to tell me.

My father remained silent, his face impassive. He knew better than to interrupt my mother.

"What?" My stomach lurched. By the way she looked at me, it was clear she wasn't about to say something uplifting.

I tried to smile, but couldn't. I'd hoped I was going to be given a tip about my future married life, perhaps a secret all married women needed to know. But by the look on her face, I knew it was unlikely.

My mother sighed. "I should have told you before now," she repeated. Her eyes looked sadly at me as she drew in a deep breath. "It's a mortal sin to refuse your husband."

With a quick peck on my cheek, she straightened her hat, turned and slipped down the aisle to take her place in the front pew. She had done her job. Her daughter was about to be married, and in white. No one could say she had failed as a mother. She had protected her daughter's virtue to the end.

Who thought up these rules? I'd never read them in the Bible. Here I was being told, I would be on a one-way trip to Hell, should I refuse my husband.

As I watched her go, my father gave a snort and mumbled something about not having had sex for years on account of my mother saying, she had finished with *all that*. As far as my mother was concerned, she had done her duty.

Knowing I was about to embark on a life of mortal sin, I stood momentarily paralysed, fear clouding the joy of my wedding day. This marriage was going to be a lot harder than I had ever imagined.

Mortal sin had once more raised its ugly head. Mortal sin lurked around every corner of my life and promised to destroy any possibility of happiness even on my wedding day.

Left with my mother's dire warning ringing in my ears, panic gripped me. I turned to my father. "I don't think I want to get married."

"Don't be silly," he said patting my hand. "It's wedding nerves."

Sex before marriage was a mortal sin, refusing sex after marriage was a mortal sin. Was there any way of escaping committing a mortal sin?

Images of my joining wives suffering the fires of Hell for having refused their husbands on account of headaches, it being the wrong time of the month, or being too tired, beset me. At that moment, I would have given anything to turn tail and run out of the chapel, down the drive, through the town and away as far as I could get.

Sensing my hesitation my father tugged at my arm and Sister Rose swung into the Wedding March.

Setting a smile on his face, he gripped my arm firmly, took a step forward and whispered desperately in my ear. "Look, everyone is waiting."

We both started the long walk down a short aisle in a crowded chapel, with Barry and Father Jerome waiting for me at the altar steps.

Sister Rose was now well into the Wedding March and people in the packed pews turned to watch my slow procession down the aisle. Some guests on the bridegroom's side of the Chapel registered momentary surprise, and I knew Barry had not told them I was black.

And so as not to disappoint our guests, I was given away, in my beautiful white wedding dress, with no struggle at all, to the man who had been responsible for my *awakening,* yet I knew, would also play a large part in my committing Mortal sins.

EPILOGUE

Although, at times I found some of my parents' beliefs amusing, I admire and love them for their fortitude in the face of racism, before, during and after the war. I thank them for their continual support and resolve in bringing me up valuing my diverse heritage. I credit my parents for making me who I am today, a confident and resilient woman determined to pass on the love I was surrounded with, my self- confidence and pride in my heritage, to my children and grandchildren.

I grew to love my mother in law and called her, Mum. We were very affectionate with each other and had lovely gossipy times together. She was a wonderful traditional English cook and concentrated on giving my daughter, her granddaughter, some of her baking secrets. She always said I was a career woman and therefore wouldn't have time to put her cooking tips to good use. And she was right. She loved her grandchildren and was very proud of them, though she never got used to my calling them or myself black. There couldn't have been a better mother in law. I still miss her and am endlessly thankful to have had her in my life.

It took me decades to forgive Sister Agatha. I knew I would be no better than her, if I did not forgive her cruelty and bigotry. She came to visit the training college I was at, in my last year of teacher training, and when told, I was there, asked to see me. On the day I was told to see her, I deliberately went out for the day. I was later told she had been dying of cancer. I felt sad I had not given her a chance to make her peace, if that was what she wanted to do? Writing this account of my experiences with her has helped me find peace and I do forgive her. In my work as a psychologist I always believed children when they divulged their abuse at the hands of another person. Sister Agatha in her antipathy to the truth, taught me to believe innocent children, as they do not know and cannot describe what happened to them unless they have personally experienced it. Although I have not and will never get over my abuse at the hands of an adult I trusted, I have learned to live with it. Thank you, Sister Agatha for your valuable lesson in trusting and believing in innocence. I believe no experience is wasted if our approach to life is positive, compassionate and forgiving.

GLOSSARY

Blarney Stone

The Blarney Stone is a block of limestone built into the battlements of Blarney
Castle, in Cork, Ireland. Legend says kissing the stone bestows the kisser with
the *'gift of the gab'* (the ability to speak smoothly, convincingly and
with confidence) .

Nigger

This is an extremely racially derogatory term (now frequently
referred to as *the n-word*), used to describe a black or dark-skinned
person.

Limbo

A *Roman Catholic belief (now defunct):* Limbo is a region on the border
between Hell and Heaven serving as the place after death where the
Souls of the unbaptised would languish
for eternity.

Mortal Sin

A *Roman Catholic belief* : A willfully committed, serious wrongdoing, the punishment being an eternity in Hell.

Original Sin

A sin that is inborn in human nature as a consequence of the sin of Adam and Eve.

Purgatory

Belief of Roman Catholics as a place in which the remorseful sinners undergo temporary Punishment.

School Milk

After the war (WW11), a1/3 of a pint of milk was given to school children daily to supplement their diet. This lasted until the 1970s.

Venial Sin

Considered a minor sin.

WOG

Western Oriental Gentleman, a disrespectful term used to refer to any nonwhite
person, especially, a dark-skinned person of Middle Eastern or Southeast
Asian origin.